DESTINED DESIRE

VAMPIRE EMBRACE ROMANCE

REGINA MORRIS

A Vampire Embrace Romance
Regina Morris
Silkhaven Publishing, LLC
Smashwords Edition

Join Regina Morris' mailing list for games, freebies, and fun at http://newsletter.reginamorris.com

Please visit author Regina Morris on her website http://www.reginamorris.com

Regina Morris enjoys connecting with fans on social media. Please find her at:
Facebook: http://www.facebook.com/ReginaAnnMorris (@ReginaMorris)

Twitter: http://www.twitter.com/ReginaMorris (@ReginaMorris)

Pinterest: http://www.pinterest.com/ReginaAnnMorris

After a car accident nearly kills his immortal father, Alexander rushes to his father's side only to discover that his parents want him to marry and stay closer to home. He's already been down this path once before with a less than desirable outcome, so he refuses. He's steadfast in his decision until his parents threaten to financially cut him off and he's forced to approach the Vampire Council for a new marriage contract.

Dionora is enjoying her new job at the Vampire Council Marriage Office. The holidays take an exciting turn for her when she discovers the next match she does is for her ex–fiancé.

Revenge is sweet with this sensual romantic comedy.

CONTENTS

Vampires Exist Among Us   ix

Chapter 1   1
Chapter 2   6
Chapter 3   11
Chapter 4   14
Chapter 5   28
Chapter 6   40
Chapter 7   46
Chapter 8   51
Chapter 9   62
Chapter 10   69
Chapter 11   77
Chapter 12   81
Chapter 13   93
Chapter 14   100
Chapter 15   108
Chapter 16   127
Chapter 17   133
Chapter 18   140
Chapter 19   144
Chapter 20   150

About the Author   165
Acknowledgments   167
Also By Regina Morris   169

Silkhaven Publishing, LLC

ISBN: 978–1–948997–16–4 (EPub ebook)

ISBN: 978–1–948997–15–7 (MOBI ebook)

ISBN: 978–1–948997–17–1 (paperback)

Library of Congress Control Number: 2018915321

DISCAIMERS:

This novel is for mature audiences only. Violence, sex, and nudity are described in this book and the target audience is for individuals 18+ years of age.

Vampire Secret Service series: Regina Morris's paranormal vampire series about a covert team of sexy vampires who protect the President of the United States. COLONY = Council Of Legalized Outlanders for National securitY

Vampire Embrace series: Regina Morris's paranormal vampires series about civilian vampires (same world as the Secret Service series but these vampires do not work for the government).

❀ Created with Vellum

VAMPIRES EXIST AMONG US

They can be our neighbor, best friend, our child's
teacher...

They alter their aged appearance based upon the amount
of blood they consume.

They move to a new area, drink a lot of blood, and appear
young. Slowly they limit their intake of blood and age,
right in front of our unsuspecting eyes.

After decades, they fake their death, move, and do it over
and over again.

CHAPTER 1

*A*lexander glared at the lovely Isabella, who sat nobly on a jeweled, wooden throne, her graceful hand gently embracing that of her husband, Salvador. Rich or not, Alexander's mother had a lot to learn about living in the modern world.

For one thing, they weren't royalty.

But she played the part beautifully. Silk gowns, expensive jewelry, and even a turned-up nose, finding everyone and everything beneath her. In truth, she ranked as one of the world's wealthiest vampires, but land and money were only meant for one thing—to pass down to your children. At least, that is what her only child firmly believed.

"An arranged marriage?" Alexander spat. "Surely, we're not about to go down that grim road again, Mother." His gaze wandered over to his father, who sat quietly but nodded in agreement with his wife's demands.

"It's time, son," Salvador said, his voice even and flat, spoken in a familiar tone. It meant: *do what your mother is asking.*

"Since my accident last year, we would like you to stay closer to home. Settle down." Salvador looked sheepishly at his only child. "A second marriage, to a woman willing to live in Italy this time, is the only way to ensure you'll stay with us. Have this union stick, and allow it to make you happy."

Marriage, stick? Yeah, his last try at marital bliss had proven sticky all right. Rich heiress, snooty family, and a nasty divorce after fulfilling his marriage contract to produce an heir—a spoiled son placed on his ex-wife's family tree. A child who didn't even speak to him.

His son was now in his fifties, still a young vampire, and off whoring around the world.

Ah, youth.

"Alexander, my dear," his mother said, her eyes filled with concern and a hint of worry. "We want only what's best for you. But we want you to come home."

He raised his arms in an effort to stop his mother. "I do come home." He glanced around the villa, a world of its own, and a family estate they'd purchased centuries ago. Human servants, if they were about, quietly fulfilled their duties and left him undisturbed in the hell he found himself in.

"I'm home now."

"Every twenty-five years..." his mother stated, her eyes narrowing in on him like she felt up to the challenge of changing his mind. "We're grateful you honor our request to spend the quarter-century holidays with us, but we want to see you more often."

Every quarter century, he stayed for Thanksgiving and Christmas, and sometimes remained until Valentine's Day or into the summer. He didn't hate being with his parents. They were wealthy, living in the most elegant homes across the world, and moving every seventy or eighty years to ensure that no one suspected their true nature.

Overall, not a bad way to live. But it wasn't *his* way.

Many vampires sated themselves with blood to retain a youthful outward appearance. Then they'd slowly adjust their blood intake so they could age gracefully, fake their deaths, and move somewhere else. It was an excellent idea, but he hated blending into the human world. Staying young. Drinking his fair share of blood and enjoying even more than his fair share of college girls who were impressed by not only his looks but also his stamina and huge wallet were more to his liking.

Alexander pointed to his father, a vampire appearing in his late twenties with raven–black hair, porcelain–white skin, and green eyes. He actually looked like Alexander's doppelganger. "Due to Father's accident, I'm home now. And it has only been three years since my last visit." Alexander glared at his father. Knowing he'd be throwing the man under the bus, but hopefully changing the subject, he asked, "Exactly how fast was your Lamborghini going?"

A wide–eyed look from Salvador to his wife, and then a stern gaze cast toward Alexander, told Alexander to change the topic—to one that would not cast Salvador in a bad light.

Alexander's mother—also looking to be in her late twenties—cleared her throat as though the car's speed had already been covered in length. "We nearly lost your father a year ago, and it took you this long to come home."

Her voice sounded sincere and tired as if the accident had taken its toll on her, as well.

Alexander stared at his parents and forced his hands to relax from the fists they were balled into. Anger would not solve anything. His parents were over two hundred years old, living in Venice, Italy and doing their best to recapture their glory days in the family's villa. If his mother weren't wearing a Victorian silk gown and a Rolex watch, and his father dressed in regal attire, sporting the latest Nike shoes, the entire scene would be archaic.

"Let me guess," Alexander said in a spiteful tone. "There's another family debt that you need me to repay by marrying someone else's horrible daughter."

His mother's face pinched with pain, for she knew how much he had suffered in his last marriage. "This time, we have no one specific in mind."

"We have placed your name on the Verheirates Schlange list with the European Vampire Council," his father said. "We want you to select from whomever they choose for you."

Not the damn list again. Alexander inwardly groaned. He should have known that his parents would do something like this. His ex–wife and nine others had been presented to him as prospective brides all those years ago, with his parents directing him to pick Bianca. He'd spent ten years in marital hell with her.

"I'm sorry, son," Salvador said. "We've made up our minds." Salvador's hand still rested within Isabella's, and his father gave his mother a sideways smile that told Alexander the two were bonded in this. "We want you here. Married, settled." Salvador took a deep breath, his chest puffing out in authority the way it always did when Alexander's father meant business. "Or you'll be financially cut off."

CHAPTER 2

*D*ionora stared at the clock on the wall and frowned. Thirty minutes until she could leave. Working at the Verheirates Schlange was not a challenging job, but it was one that could consume the day and leave you feeling hollow inside.

Finding mates for lonely vampires. Potentially a great career, but she had placed herself—for not just the first or second time—on the damn list. This was now her third attempt. Eight years had already passed since the last placement, and still, there was no mate for her. Of course, her family wasn't wealthy. She held no land or title. And she didn't even have any special ability like some vampires did. She remained a plain Jane.

Dionora stared at the computer on her desk, which showed all her completed tasks. She had personally arranged for twenty couples to meet this week—to perhaps fall in love. Not bad for it only being a Wednesday. Some of the pairings were a great fit, while others probably wouldn't make it down the aisle. The result wasn't up to her. She only made the matches.

Even the calendar and whiteboard along the wall showed nothing left for her to do today. But she needed to run down the clock for another half hour before she could leave. She smelled the freshly brewed dark roast from the outer office, so she walked to the coffee bar with her new Christmas mug, given to her at the most recent holiday party, and poured herself a cup. Other than alcohol, coffee was the only human drink she enjoyed.

She noticed the lit Christmas tree, and since she and her officemate were the only two left in the office, she unplugged the fake six-foot Douglas Fir. She also turned off the soft Christmas music that played in the background.

She then walked back to her desk and took a seat. The old chair gave way and creaked as she leaned back. The office wasn't grand, and the job didn't have prestige, but being home for the holidays felt wonderful, especially since she temporarily stayed with her parents.

Her officemate, Margo, stood from her desk and walked to the large, third-story picture window that overlooked the town. "It's snowing." Margo's voice sounded excessively enthusiastic, but then Dionora had recently moved to France from Canada and snow had lost its appeal a long time ago.

"I love tracking people in the fresh snow." A guttural sound escaped from the back of Margo's throat in what Dionora assumed was anticipation of the vampire's next meal. "Too bad you're manning the fort and can't take off for the holidays." Margo's voice sounded sarcastic, and

Dionora knew the woman didn't care that Dionora had to work while everyone else had time off.

Dionora ignored the comment and focused on shutting down her computer. Her new job meant new responsibilities and a new learning curve. Margo had worked here for years and knew all the insandouts of the Verheirates Schlangelist. Grateful for the job, and more importantly the money and blood bank she enjoyed, Dionora still wished she had some vacation time during the holidays. A husband and kids would be even nicer.

"The humans never see you coming," Margo continued as she licked her lips in anticipation of the hunt.

Dionora never should have shared with Margo that she didn't enjoy biting people for food. Now, it was the butt of every office joke.

She suddenly felt a pang of hunger herself. Being a poor vampire, living paycheck to paycheck just to get by, and working with a surly co–worker hadn't been part of Dionora's childhood dream, but fate had a way of messing with you. At the very least, staying with her parents was helping her out financially until she could get a place of her own.

"I love this time of year," Margo said, glancing out the window to the Eiffel tower in the distance. "Vacationers and drunk partygoers." Margo licked her lips, her fangs showing slightly.

Dionora didn't consider herself a prude, but hunting humans had never sat well with her. She felt guilty drinking from them directly, and to be honest, she'd never been that great at compelling them to forget their meal-time donation to her. "The Vampire Council gives us plenty of bagged blood, Margo."

"Bagged." Margo's face creased as if she tasted something bad. "Easy, but not as delicious."

The hunting rules in Europe and Asia were far more relaxed than in other countries, so Dionora allowed the remark to pass. She was new to this office and this continent, having lived in North America for the last fifteen years.

Dionora's computer beeped as she was about to close down her email, causing her to stare down at the flashing screen. "What does a priority code one mean?"

Margo turned, her gaze now upon the computer, her eyes wide. "Priority one?" She crossed the tiny space of the office and stood behind Dionora to read the screen. "It means drop everything and find this desperate soul a mate ASAP." She leaned in to get a better view of the screen. "It's usually some lame–ass vampire who has money to burn and thinks expediting things will yield better results."

Margo rolled her eyes. "Like they'll get extra–special treatment when they're a loser themselves."

The sounds of Dionora clicking on the keyboard filled the room as she ignored Margo's jaded comments. She opened the client file attached to the email and saw the surname *Marino* in large letters across the top.

It can't be, she thought, her chest tightening. Her fingers trembled as she opened the claim and read the name *Alexander*.

No, no, no.

The air escaped her lungs, and she felt the sting of her fangs as they descended and poked her tongue. She knew this family, especially Alexander. Mutual friends had told her that he had last been seen in Spain and seemed determined to run amok without a care in the world. Evidently, her friends had been misinformed. The rotten bastard was actually trying for a second chance at marital bliss. A guilty pleasure tugged at Dionora'sheart. *I hope his ex–wife tore out his heart,* she thought.

"Nice!" Margo said, the excitement spilling from her voice as she continued to read over Dionora's shoulder. "Respectable family, old lineage." Dionora saw Margo'seyes widen in the reflection of her computer screen before Margo's lips curled upward into a smile as she continued to read. "Rich, too."

Margo leaned in more and stood close enough that she was nearly breathing down Dionora's neck.

"I'm supposed to start my holiday and won't be back until after the New Year." Margo read more of the file. "But I'll postpone everything a few days so I can work with you on this vampire's list of potential brides. We'll need to check the database, select five prospects, contact the client, and set up interviews…"

"You don't have to cancel your vacation, Margo." An evil smirk crossed Dionora's face. "I know the procedure." A bubble of excitement tingled up Dionora's spine. She knew exactly what to do to get back at her ex–fiancé.

CHAPTER 3

*A*lexander waved the flight attendant away after she had served him his Bloody Mary. Once she left, he took out a small flask and poured some A+ blood into the glass, happy that he could compel airline security to ignore the security infraction. "The marriage notice came within hours," he complained to Stephan, his best friend and travel companion. "Only fucking hours."

Stephan finished his drink and picked up the new one left by the flight attendant, also adding a splash of blood. "I say screw your parents. Let's enjoy the time we have in Paris."

"No." Alexander let out a sigh of surrender. "This time, my parents mean business."

Alexander often got his way, but not when his parents teamed up and worked against him. Bank accounts would be shut off; Alexander's way of life harder to preserve. He needed to play it cool and find another solution. In any event, he would make sure there was no marriage in his near future.

Not after the last bridal fiasco.

"So, how is this expedited list going to work?" Stephan scratched his head and looked thoughtful as if remembering the process they had undergone before. "Is it different from the last time?"

Alexander glanced around, making sure no one could eavesdrop. In a high–pitched voice that only vampires could hear, he said, "I get to select one of five candidates. A scheduled interview to share personal family details is set up, finances arranged…and in the end, more land and money are combined, allowing both families to prosper. So, instead of the usual ten candidates, I'm getting half as many to choose from, and I have to make a decision quickly." His voice trailed off in scorn. "God, I don't need another child. I still have my placement in my family line but…" He thought of his last marriage and the contract. "Sometimes, the wife's family line is fulfilled first."

"Can't you just reject all the women and call it a day?" Stephan gulped the last of his drink. "They need to make these glasses bigger," he said, holding up the small container, his eyes glinting at the seeming stupidity of such a small amount.

Alexander ignored the comment, although he felt the same about the drinks. "My parents made it clear I must pick one of the prospective brides. *And* I must earnestly interview and meet her." His eyebrow raised. "But what happens after that, well…that is all up to me."

"Sabotage." His friend's eyes lit up. "On paper, you're rich, handsome, and still have a place in your family tree. Other than having no special abilities that would make you a god on that list, what are you going to do?"

There were many plans brewing inside Alexander's

head, but he managed to say, "Play the part of the whoring bastard."

"Not much of a stretch."

"A woman who still believes in arranged marriages will be from a proper family, and they'll expect their future son–in–law to follow certain protocols. I have to be someone no family will accept. They'll reject me, my vow to my family will be honored, and we'll be free to roam." He took a deep breath, and then his face lit up. "Let's go to Rome. We haven't been there in a while."

"You know, you could get lucky and get a bad list of women to choose from."

"Lucky?" Alexander shifted in the tiny seat, his knees knocking into the tray table in front of him and causing the glasses to clink together.

"Pick the most questionable person on the list and have *your* family reject *her*. That way, you'll know you're safe." Stephen twisted in his seat and stared Alexander directly in the eyes. "The women on the list may be desperate and choose anyone for financial gain. You need to play your cards right. You need to be in control of the rejection."

The plan was clear. Alexander would have to be the one at the helm.

"There is a time penalty for rejecting a chosen mate. My name, no matter how much money my parents throw at the damn process, will be placed on a waitlist for another ten years if the marriage contract falls through." Alexander's determined voice held a plan. "Yes. I know exactly what to do."

CHAPTER 4

"*T*hat's bullshit, Margo." Dionora shook her head as she looked at the list of the five candidates for Alexander's bridal selection displayed on the computer screen. She now understood why Margo had agreed to have Dionora make the list of candidates... because *she* was going to have final approval.

"I made this list last night with a particular client in mind." Dionora pointed to the fifth and last name on the list, a last-minute write-in. "You can't put your name on this vampire's list of potential brides."

Margo was tall, thin, and absolutely gorgeous, the exact type that Dionora had painstakingly left *off* the list of choices for Alexander. Everyone listed was supposed to be undesirable to Alexander, but having Margo as a potential would mean that he had at least one good option.

Dionora couldn't allow it.

"You're only upset because I replaced you on the list," Margo said, sounding very authoritative and decisive.

God, Margo actually believed that Dionora wanted to marry that bastard. Dionora's pride was bruised, and she was offended at just the thought. The only reason she had placed herself on the list was because she knew that Alexander wouldn't pick her. And, if he did, she was going to dump his ass the first chance she got.

"I've worked my butt off at this company for nearly fifteen years." Margo stood straighter and narrowed her eyes more defiantly. "One of the perks of working here is finding a husband, and this Alexander looks like the perfect catch."

Perfect on paper? Yes. But Dionora knew differently. "Trust me on this one. He is a whoring bastard."

Margo placed her hands on her hips, narrowed her gaze, and stared at Dionora. "So you place your name on a whoring bastard's list?" Margo nodded her head as she studied Dionora. "You look younger today."

Dionora usually allowed herself to look in her thirties since humans tended to treat her more as an adult that way, as opposed to when she looked as young as twenty-two—the age she'd been when she transitioned into a vampire. This morning, though, she'd drunk enough blood to look in her late twenties. Dionora glared at Margo, who had obviously done the same thing. "Like you haven't lost a few years yourself."

"I'm your superior, and the list stays as is." Under her breath, Margo mumbled, "I'm not going to have the new girl in the office keep me from catching this man."

The plan would fail. Dionora's breakfast threatened to come back up. Alexander wanted to find a bride, and every potential on that original list was a horror show. Plan A was for Alexander to reject the entire list and get slammed with a ten-year penalty. Plan B was for him to pick *her*, and then Dionora would get the revenge she had waited so long for—and the rejection would be a public display. Something grand.

But now, everything was ruined. There was a dead ringer listed. Margo was an impressive vampire, and Dionora knew Alexander would pick her.

Damn it.

Margo was blond and model-perfect. A bitch, but from a good family with moderate money. She also knew how to play men. In the last few weeks, Dionora had seen her go out on several dates. Fake smiles, fake sincerity, and probably fake orgasms. Anything to land a man.

"Print the files," Margo ordered. "My future husband will be here soon." Margo swaggered out of the office on her four-inch heels, her designer suit fitting perfectly.

After waiting decades for her revenge, Dionora wasn't going to miss her chance. Plan A may fall through, but Plan B was still viable. She printed the information about the women and even the dossier on herself. It was a long shot that Alexander would pick her over Margo, but there was still a chance.

Dionora undid the top button of her dress and allowed some more cleavage to show. A fresh dab of bright red lipstick also wouldn't hurt.

She placed six manila folders on the desk in front of her. Five vampire women who wanted a man, and then her own file. She'd been told she couldn't alter the list, but that didn't mean she couldn't amend it. She now understood why Margo seemed happy to see the losers on the list. She had planned to put herself on it.

The bitch.

Dionora would get even with Alexander one way or the other. Even if he married Margo, he wouldn't be happy. The woman was overly demanding and had zero charisma.

Thinking about all the women who worked in the office, and the high turnaround for the jobs, Dionora suspected that most women worked here just to find a man.

Pathetic.

Finding a husband to marry and have kids with? Sure. That was on Dionora's agenda. But, *needing* a man? She had always felt that a woman, vampire or not, should be self-sufficient and never rely on a man to complete her.

She had even felt that way when engaged to Alexander.

So why was she applying lipstick and feeling as if butterflies were crawling inside her stomach trying violently to break free?

The queasiness must be because she hadn't seen or spoken to Alexander since he'd left her nearly at the altar decades ago. He was only a man. A male who deserved what he was about to get.

And yet, she'd drunk heavily this morning and brought her aged appearance down to look her best for the man. She'd even put on a dress. He favored the color red, and that's exactly what color the dress was. And she never wore dresses. She preferred jeans, especially in winter.

God, she was desperate for her plan to work.

When Margo reentered the office with her bra stuffed to accentuate her breasts, Dionora realized that she wasn't as desperate as some.

The office doorbell rang, and she knew Alexander

would be escorted to her office within minutes. She figured he'd be alone, no need to bring the parents. Dionora felt her eyes shift from their normal blue hue to a heated vampire black. Her fangs also sprang forth. She hated Alexander's fucking parents. She wasn't good enough to join their family? Well, fuck them.

She took some calming breaths to relax and settle her vampire nature. This was no hunt, only a decisive kill. There was no need for anger. She held all the cards, and Alexander was going to get screwed.

A tap sounded at the door, followed by the receptionist's voice. "Miss Margo, I have your client, Alexander Marino, and his companion, Stephan, to see you."

Dionora's ears perked up. Stephan came, too? She hadn't seen that weasel since leaving Italy.

"Please, show them in," Margo said in a singsong voice. She stared daggers at Dionora. "I'll do all the talking."

The receptionist opened the door. "This way, gentlemen."

And that's when Dionora saw Alexander. Jet–black hair framed his porcelain–white skin. His boyish good looks were offset by the scruff of a beard. Decades may have passed, but the man could still take her breath away. Tall and muscular, sure, but the vampire reeked of sex appeal and manliness that could cause any woman's core to moisten. She felt her knees grow weak, and she was still sitting.

"Gentlemen," Margo said with the biggest smile imaginable on her face. "Please, come in." She shook their hands. "My name is Margo, and I'm your relationship coordinator. This,"—her hand waved in Dionora's direction—"is my assistant."

Assistant my ass. Despite Dionora's low position and no power as the newest hire in the office, she was nobody's assistant. She ignored the insult and stood from her chair, a power move she had learned years ago. Besides, she didn't need to be eye–level with Alexander's crotch, no matter how talented the man was in bed.

She held out her hand to greet the men and allowed them to cross the room to meet her at her desk. With a dismissive, "That will be all," she politely ordered the receptionist from the room, even though she had asked about refreshments. Placing a stoic pleased–to–meet–you grin on her face, she offered the men seats before Margo could.

No refreshments. No niceties. No pleasant caseworker to deal with.

Alexander would get the raw treatment, and straight from her.

"Dionora?"

Alexander's voice sounded like pure honey: silky–smooth, sweet, and dripping with appeal.

His face beamed with surprise as his gaze perused her from head to toe. It was a look she figured he gave most of his past lovers when bumping into any of the masses that had shared his bed.

His dark hair, piercing green eyes, and that smile of his…the one that could always melt her heart. They were the tools he used to make any woman fall for him.

But the smile was fleeting. It only lasted a second. Alexander looked away and pointed to the nameplate on her desk, his fingers tracing her name. "I didn't know you worked here," he said in a low tone.

He looked nervous. He was never nervous. He turned to Stephan. "You remember Stephan, right?"

How could she forget? The three of them had grown up in Venice together. Played together. Went to school together. They were the three fucking Musketeers for Heaven's sake—until they deemed her unworthy for being a poor village vampire.

"It's good to see you again." Stephan stood and stretched across the desk to hug her, but she leaned away and stopped the intrusion. This was business, not a reunion of old friends.

Stephan looked the same. Blond hair, brown eyes, and glued to Alexander's hip. Being shorter in build than Alexander, the vampire had always—literally and figuratively—looked up to Alexander as a big brother.

"You all know each other?" Margo asked in a Southern belle's well–I–do–declare type of way.

"We grew up together," Stephan said through gritted teeth. Having Dionora refuse a hug had obviously hurt him, but she didn't care. Stephan had abandoned her long ago.

Margo gave Dionora a side glance that was filled with hatred. But Margo was just one more person in the room who wasn't Dionora's favorite at the moment, although she did rank the least vile of the three.

"Well, we know why we're here, and this isn't your first time dealing with the Verheirates Schlange, so let's get started," Dionora said.

When Alexander didn't make eye contact, she asked, "Are you ready, Mr. Marino?"

He stared at her, then glanced at Margo and then back to Dionora. "Let's get this over with."

Margo had given Dionora a look of contempt when the men gathered around Dionora's desk and not hers, but Dionora planned to run this show. Plus, these were old friends. There was no way she'd let Margo handle this case.

Dionora ignored Margo, who now hovered behind her. "I have the selection for you."

"I think you'll be pleased by what we have found for you," Margo held out her hands so Dionora could place the files in them. Margo seemed desperate to take control, but that wasn't a part of Dionora's plan.

Margo cleared her throat and tried, once again, to get Dionora to hand over the folders. "These five selections—"

"These five are the vampire women we've selected for you," Dionora interrupted sharply, holding tightly to all the folders. She opened the first one and slid it across the table. A huge, glossy image of a vampire woman now stared up at Alexander, and Dionora eyed him as he carefully viewed the picture.

"Straight to business, then," Alexander said, regaining his composure. His gaze immediately went to the picture of a blond vampire woman with piercing, blue eyes. "Helga Schmidt?"

"German. Strong family lines. Prestige. Some money." Dionora's determined voice uttered each description sharply, but it nearly quivered over the word *money*. It was wartime Nazi money. All intimate family details had to be revealed in the report, even the most unseemly. "She worked as an officer at Auschwitz–Birkenau. Her family benefited from the suffering of the millions of Jews she helped to slaughter."

"Really?" Alexander gave a side–glance at Stephan. "Slaughtered Jews."

"And she's looking for a husband?" Stephan said.

Margo shrugged. "Everyone wants to find love. The Verheirates Schlange takes that into consideration with our clientele, no matter what their past is."

"Let's just say that her family would likely be locked away if they were human and still alive following the war," Dionora said, interrupting Margo and keeping control. "Being a vampire, she can compel people to forget her war crimes." Dionora now pointed to the financial section of the report. "She's struggling financially now since there isn't an occupation for her or a country to overthrow anymore."

"I see that." Alexander closed the folder, his face creased with an unease that caused a moment of excitement for Dionora. "Let's take a look at the next one, shall we?"

"Of course," Margo said, holding out her hand but getting nothing.

Dionora opened the next one in the same fashion she had the first and slid the folder in front of Alexander. "Fanny Mae Russle. Floridian in the USA. Gator farmer and taxidermist. The family is quite wealthy."

Alexander stared at the picture of the female, her handsome features much more suited to a man than a woman. "She has a missing hand?"

"Gator bite from ten years ago." Margo pointed at the paperwork. The image didn't show the missing hand, but the comments below the picture did.

Dionora took her right hand and indicated just above her left wrist where the woman's hand had been severed.

"She's been looking for a mate for the past twenty–some years. Wants to say in the States, too. Special ability is that she can pick up thoughts from those who are close to her."

"Mind reading?" Stephan said, his lips pursed in what looked like fear and utter disgust. "That would be entertaining."

"The family would be very excited to have this placement. Fanny Mae is the youngest daughter in a very close family. They're eager for more grandchildren," Margo explained.

"Okay, then." Alexander's pause told Dionora that the list had brought out the exact reaction that both she and Margo were hoping for.

"Excellent choices." Alexander now gazed at the third folder, one more in a string of what Dionora could only hope was the most pathetic list in the world for future brides.

Dionora slid the third folder across the table. "Candace Overton. Somewhat of a shut–in. She suffers from agoraphobia."

Stephan's eyebrow rose. "Isn't that the fear of leaving one's home?"

"She hasn't left her modest three–bedroom house in Nebraska for the last fifty years. She's also somewhat of a hoarder." Dionora pointed to the picture. "That's her in a woman's leisure suit from the seventies, boxes of clutter lying in the background of the image. That's a recent picture of her."

Alexander stared at the plaid outfit. "Quite retro." He closed the folder. "Next?"

Opening the fourth folder, Dionora said, "This circus performer—"

Alexander waved his hand across the folder and didn't allow it to be set in front of him. "Next."

Remaining in her hands were the last two folders. Dionora glanced up at Margo, whose reddened face and pursed lips had twisted, her features morphing into something impatient and unattractive—especially since there should only be one folder left, not two.

Dionora opened Margo's file and slid it across the table. "This is Margo Weston's file."

Margo's hand went to her chest, and a smile appeared on her face. "Seems like the database fancied us together." She sat on the desk, crossed her legs, and leaned in. "My name popping up surprised me, but it does look like we're a good match."

If Margo touched her hair one more time, Dionora swore she'd vomit.

Gently touching her file, Margo added, "My family has done well financially. I've never been married, no children."

Dionora studied Alexander's reaction. His goofy smile, his stupid comments...he actually liked Margo as a possibility.

And Stephan was no better. He couldn't take his eyes off Margo's legs.

Shit. The last thing Dionora wanted to do was set Alexander up with someone good.

"I have to say, I'm impressed." Alexander stared at Margo's body, so she stood and did a little twirl for him, his gaze taking in her backside as she spun.

"Very nice." He gave a nod to Stephan. "What do you think?"

"Good on paper. Good in person."

Dionora cleared her throat. "There is one more profile, call it a bonus one." This was the moment.

She slid the last file over and opened the folder slowly, knowing he'd probably laugh and then pick Margo—blowing Dionora's chance to get revenge.

Her eight-by-ten, glossy image stared up at Alexander.

"You?" Alexander's eyes widened—not with anger, but with surprise. "You're on my list?"

God, his voice was sexy and deep. So much so, that she almost didn't catch the underlying insult.

Why *shouldn't* she be on a prestigious listing for a vampire who had money? She was marriage-worthy, not riff-raff. She had been listed on Alexander's first Verheirates Schlange because very few vampires lived in Venice at the time, and the process was manually done with no help from a computer. Now, thanks to the internet, the selection process was worldwide. But she *was* worthy.

Bile bubbled up her throat, and she regretted drinking so much blood this morning. "The computer made the selection, not me," she lied. "Seems that we have much in common: growing up in Venice, same age, and we still have room on our family trees for children."

Yes, on paper, she looked fine, but she didn't mention the finances or the fact that she was still a poor village vampire, at least according to him and his family.

Margo stood and said nothing. Oh, she'd probably tell Dionora later that she was fired, but that wasn't now, and it would have to come from their boss, not from Margo.

Not that it mattered. Getting even with Alexander seemed worth Dionora's career. Pairing Alexander with

Margo and her plastic personality would not be enough revenge. Dionora wanted to reject him.

Alexander picked up the pages from the folder, placing Dionora's picture down. He read the contents carefully, and she knew the personal information he gleaned. She had hoped he'd close the file and be done with it, but no... He kept reading.

A minute later, he was still reading. Dionora could tell by the look in Margo's eyes that she was not happy. Alexander had only glanced at Margo'spicture, he had not read her file. He picked up each page of Dionora's dossier and read each one carefully.

She felt bare and naked in front of him and flashed Stephan, who sat quietly studying Alexander, a nervous smile.

Finally, Alexander placed the papers back into the folder and shut it. He cupped his chin with his hand and quietly tapped the folder as though deep in thought. His gaze was distant, and silence continued to fill the room.

Alexander had always been a serious thinker. Looking at him now, he was just as handsome as she remembered him. His hair was shorter, and he had the scruff of a beard, but his brilliant green eyes were mesmerizing against his pale skin. He was gorgeous.

She thought back to the many times they had been alone in her family's barn with him above her, her thighs straddling his strong hips as he repeatedly thrust into her.

She crossed her legs and tried to ignore the tightening sensation she felt. He could still drench her panties, and she needed to be careful. He may have been her first crush, her first kiss, her first lover...but he was also the one who had left her.

She couldn't let him—or his looks—get into her head…or into anything further south, no matter how handsome he looked.

"Quite the list," he said at last, pointing to all the folders.

"I'm glad you're pleased." Margo's gaze drifted to the six folders. "As you know, your family has expedited these proceedings."

The look Alexander gave Margo told Dionora that he was either constipated or unhappy with the circumstances and the selection.

Dionora hoped the look was for both.

"Normally, the Council allows a month for a decision to be made, but your parents have asked for a quick resolution." Dionora eyed him with a wry smile. "We can supply these folders electronically for you, but we do ask that you make your decision by tomorrow morning."

Alexander's gaze shifted to her, and Dionora detected a hint of worry in his eyes as a bead of sweat pooled on his temple. He stared deeply into her eyes. "Please make the arrangements with Stephan." He stood and quickly left her office.

That's when Dionora noticed that he'd left with her file.

CHAPTER 5

*A*lexander sat in the back of the dimly lit pub, his butt falling into the downward bend of a well-worn and stained booth. He would prefer to sit at the bar on one of the wooden bar stools, but the large mirror behind the bartender picked up his fuzzy reflection. Potentially, it could draw some unwanted attention from the humans, and he didn't need anything else on his plate at the moment.

He tapped his foot nervously against the brass rail of the table. Picking up his eighth vodka shot, Alexander stared at Dionora's folder one more time before downing the drink.

His rubbery knees had gained solidity once more, and his heart no longer pounded so loudly that he could hear it. But the whirring of the blenders filled with icy concoctions, and the people talking in the crowded pub could have added to the latter.

After all these years, he now knew where Dionora was. She lived here, in Paris. The city made for lovers.

His fist tightened around the shot glass, and he accidentally crushed it, causing shards of glass to cut into his hand.

He could still feel pain. Which meant he needed more to drink.

Not wanting to get up, he waved to the bartender. The busy vampire stood behind the counter, avoiding the mirror as well, his sleeves rolled up as he clinked clean glassware together at the tiny sink. Alexander gestured a second time and got his attention. The bartender nodded, and Alexander knew five more shots of the magic forget-her elixir was coming. It was what he liked to call the "Dionora Special." Straight vodka until he passed out and forgot what she looked like. His favorite drink over the years.

He pulled out his pocket watch and opened the casing. There, crushed against the lid, was the only picture of him and Dionora he had. The image had been taken during the time of early photography, but was not a tin-plated photograph. The worn paper had whitened along the edges over the years, but the two of them smiling had been the only physical reminder he had of them together.

The picture had been taken before their transitioning years; before the camera could no longer capture their images. Dionora had complained of the heat that hot summer day, saying that her sweat matted down her hairdo. He found the image sexy. Her tresses resembled her bedroom hair after having made love to him, their passions causing her skin to glisten with perspiration and flattening her hair—just like in this black–and–white picture.

Alexander studied Dionora'simage. They had both

been so young. Her virgin curves, the innocent gaze in her eyes, and the hopefulness in her heart. Even though he too had been inexperienced in love, he had taken her virginity. In the few years they were together, they had experimented and pleasured each other in various ways, mastering what the other wanted. He couldn't get enough of her.

He hadn't been prepared to see her again and had certainly not been ready to sit across a desk from her and talk about future brides.

Even just shaking her hand had gotten him half-hard.

A barmaid arrived with his drinks. Oddly, she—just like the bartender—was a vampire. Alexander had detected them the second he walked into the place since the tiny hairs on the back of his neck had stood on end, telling him that another predator was nearby. But, like most vampires he had bumped into in the past, as long as you didn't show any hostility toward them, you were welcome.

Alexander placed more money on the table and then gulped one of the drinks.

God, Dionora had not only looked fantastic, but she also smelled incredible with a strong scent of lilacs coming from her. And the dress she wore? Back in the day, it would have been considered a slip. He could tell that she wasn't wearing a bra, and the dress had way too little fabric to disguise her pert nipples. He'd done everything he could not to stare at them, even though they were pointed at him and begging to be touched.

"There you are." Stephan walked up to the booth and took a seat. "You're lucky I'm such a good tracker."

"I knew you'd find me." Alexander closed the watch and placed it back into his pocket. "This is the closest bar to the Council offices, it couldn't have been that hard to track me down."

Stephan studied the number of empty shot glasses in front of Alexander. "Not the Dionora Special."

"And why not? My God, she's just down the road, trying to coordinate my next wedding." Alexander downed another shot, realizing that he needed to order another round now that Stephan was here.

Stephan grouped the glasses together and then placed his phone down before downing one of the drinks. "These ladies are whack jobs just wanting husbands." He shivered as he pointed to his phone. "I got all their files. Florida gal and mind reading. They're all nightmares."

He then pointed to Dionora's file on the table. "Except for Dionora. I've always liked her." He gave his friend a serious look, one filled with nostalgia. "You two should have been married all those years ago."

Alexander's heart had raced since stepping foot into that room and seeing her again. If Stephan or Dionora had picked up on his anxiety with their vampire hearing, he hoped they assumed it was because of the excitement of the list selection and not at his surprise of finding the only woman he'd ever truly loved trying to match him up with others. Margo would have also picked up on his anxiety, but he didn't care what she thought about him.

Alexander downed another shot, and an old memory flashed in his head. He and Dionora had stopped at a tavern, much like this one, but where the innkeeper offered rooms on the second level. Alexander had rented

31

one of the suites, and he and Dionora had enjoyed a night like no other.

Alexander had enjoyed her body in many ways that night, but he'd always remember her ankles lifted high, her bare folds open to him, and the pleasure on her face as he took her repeatedly.

"She looked amazing today," Stephan said, interrupting Alexander's trip down memory lane. "I had forgotten how beautiful her blue eyes and long brunette hair are. Plus, she looked smoking hot in that outfit."

A smile crept across Stephan's face, and Alexander was sure he had noticed the lack of any undergarments under her dress today, as well. Alexander raised a finger in protest. "Watch it. That's Dionora you're talking about."

Stephan's hands went up in submission, and he seemingly decided to get the bartender's attention. Taking a good look at the vampire behind the bar, Stephan grabbed Alexander's arm and nodded for him to take a look. "Do you recognize the bartender?"

Alexander positioned his head so he could see past Stephan. "Should I?"

Stephan turned back around and faced his friend, his eyes as wide as Alexander had ever seen them. "Of all the bars in Paris, you have to drink at the one where Dionora's brother works?"

No way that was Dionora's brother. Alexander craned his neck around and took a better look. Same brunette hair, same pale skin... Finally, his shoulders slumped. "Shit. It *is* him. I'm pretty sure he hates me, too." He gazed down at the empty shot glasses. "How much spit do you think I've drunk tonight?"

"No more than usual." Stephan gave him a determined look and whispered, "You haven't said anything about this list that he could have overheard, did you?"

"What? Me?" Alexander shook his head, but tried to remember. "I didn't say anything."

They watched as the bartender finished cleaning the glasses and wiping down the bar. He disappeared for a minute into the other room, but then came back wearing a coat.

"Looks like he's leaving." Stephan caught the attention of the barmaid and ordered another round. "What the hell was his name?"

"Edmund." He was a good ten years older than Dionora and had always been a pain in Alexander's side, even before the breakup. Overprotective and domineering...but he always had his heart in the right place.

Stephan nodded slowly. "I always hated him. He was a bully and used to tease me relentlessly."

"Are you sure that was Edmund?" Alexander shoved all the empty glasses to one side of the table so the barmaid could pick them up.

"I'm positive."Stephan showed his bare arm to Alexander. "This scar came from him when he convinced me to help with the new crop machine during the harvest one time."

"Edmund wasn't a big fan of mine either. He always made sure that Dionora and I never had a moment alone." Thinking back to their courtship, Alexander realized just how much Edmund had done to keep him away from Dionora.

Thinking it was probably best not to talk about him or

Dionora's family in a bar where Edmund worked, Alexander changed the topic. "Margo had an exciting body."

Alexander was sure even pretending to be interested in Margo didn't help to hide his true feelings about Dionora from Stephan—or from Dionora.

"What are you going to do?" Stephan asked, his drinks arriving. Alexander ordered another round for himself.

Alexander studied the shot glasses and couldn't see any spit in them. "The list used to be for proper women looking for mates to enrich their lives and family lines." He shook his head in disgust. "Now, it seems that all the desperate women are making a play for men." He eyed the phone questioningly, knowing the device contained the list. "Is this the best a computer could select for me? I mean, really?" His hand waved in front of his body, and he shook his head. "It's quite shameful that you can't rely on software these days. I mean, Margo seemed lovely, but…"

Stephan downed one of his shots. "I'm pretty sure you didn't meet Margo today, although she did look hot."

Alexander nodded to the phone. "You think we met an actress?"

"No. I think she won't show her true colors until after the 'I dos' are said, and you're stuck with her." He placed his empty shot glass upside down on the table and began to neatly stack his empties. "She's already lied to you."

The barmaid came and collected the glasses, pausing to wipe down the table.

Alexander's hand touched the smoothness of Dionora's folder, and he waited for the woman to leave. "Margo has already lied to me? How so?"

Stephan gave him an are–you–kidding–me glance. "How many women does the selection usually have?"

"Five."

"And you were offered six." He shook his head as though it were a no–brainer. "Do the math."

"They said the sixth candidate was a bonus."

Stephan leaned in and looked him squarely in the eyes. "Are you already drunk? Spend some neurons on this one."

Alexander paused and thought about the bonus pick, and then the answer occurred to him. "Margo added herself to my list."

"Bingo." Stephan sat back in the booth, obviously pleased that Alexander had figured it out.

"But Dionora's folder was the last one. Maybe she added *herself* to my list."

A blank expression appeared on Stephan's face. "With your history, do you really think she would voluntarily place herself on your selection list so you could reject her a second time?"

No, that wouldn't make any sense. She'd never put herself at risk of being hurt again. At least not by taking a chance with him. He'd have to focus on the others in the list.

"I can't pick Margo. My parents wouldn't reject her, and I'd be stuck in a marriage."

"You can't take the Nazi or the crazy croc lady." Stephan shook his head, his body shivering as if the thought were too horrid to think about.

"And the shut–in or the circus freak?" Alexander nervously laughed. "I've never seen such a lineup before." He glanced across the room and found the barmaid. "That

35

vampire who's been serving me drinks is better than most on my list."

He studied the young woman. "Hardworking, probably living paycheck to paycheck." His eyes lit up. "I could throw the entire list away and just ask her to marry me. My parents could reject her instead."

"That's not a good idea." Stephan studied the woman. "I think I see a wedding ring on her finger."

When Alexander cocked his head for a better look, Stephan added, "Besides, if you toss the list out and choose a love match instead of a Council match, the contractual obligations have longer timelines."

Alexander nodded and sat back in the booth. "Then we pick from my pathetic list. We just need to make sure that whomever I pick rejects me."

The barmaid came back to the table where she cleared the empties and asked if they needed anything. With a dismissive wave of Stephan's hand, she left.

"Alexander, the only option is—" Stephan said just above a whisper.

"The only option is Dionora," Alexander whispered and cut him off, knowing but dreading the truth. "And my family already rejected her once." The past love of his life or not, he suspected that Dionora hated him. The Verheirates Schlange list had been easier to manage back in the day. Fewer vampires. Fewer choices. Fewer disappointments. Selecting her back then and then rejecting her had shaken her family, and they all saw him as the enemy.

"Given your history with her, and the way things turned out,"—Stephan gave his friend a questioning glance—"does it seem wise to choose her?"

Alexander thought about his past and what he had brought upon her household, a then-poor family who had hopes and dreams of marrying off their only daughter to a wealthy line. If Alexander knew anything about his past love, he knew she wasn't a shrinking violet. The skinned knees and roughhousing they had done as children, the pacts they had made, and the broken promises had only strengthened her into a career woman of today.

A sexy and independent female who had no real need of a husband. No man was needed to protect her now. No man needed to shower her with loyalty and devotion. No man needed to complete her. And yet, she sought a husband.

"Alexander?" Stephan snapped his fingers in front of Alexander's eyes to catch his attention.

Alexander felt as if time were against him, and a decision had to be made. There was only one thing to do.

"Dionora is perfect," he said, his voice shaky with speculation. The dossier on her that he'd just read gave him a brief understanding of her world. She was a traveler, a scholar, and not the fresh-faced innocent lass of their youth. The report never mentioned a marriage, though. It was customary to never mention ex-boyfriends, fiancés, or betrothals either. Surely, she had gained experience and wisdom with men.

Experience with men. The thought haunted him. Decades had passed, and she was a rare beauty. She must have had a slew of men in her bed.

"The family is still quite plain. Not much to offer as a dowry. No land. No sizeable possessions," Stephan said, carefully opening Dionora's file and reading it in a hushed tone.

Alexander snatched the folder from Stephan's hand, cradling it against his chest. Regardless of what had happened between Alexander and Dionora, the information in the file would remain only with him. "Do not read her dossier on your phone, either."

"Aren't you being a bit overprotective?"

"You will honor her privacy." Alexander's voice sounded definitive as he glanced at the paper folder in front of him. Everything he needed to know about her existed in her file. Everything but how she felt about being on his selection list.

After several minutes, Stephan said, "I think it's best to stick to the known commodity."

Stephan had made it sound as dispassionate as picking stocks and bonds. This was so much more personal, and Alexander hadn't thought that choosing a bride for his parents to reject would be so difficult. But he hadn't known Dionora would be on his list.

He didn't even want to get married.

"The choice is clear. If I choose Dionora, she has an opportunity to cast me aside." Alexander gulped down a drink, feeling rather pleased with himself. "I rather like that. It allows her and her family to get even with me."

"And if she doesn't turn you down?"

Alexander didn't like the idea of a second rejection for Dionora, but she'd at least see it coming. "Then my family will reject her, and the Council will suspend me from the Verheirates Schlange list for ten years as a penalty. We can go on our merry way, with my finances still in place for at least another decade."

Stephan's face lit up. "Excellent choice. But what if

neither party says no. Are you prepared to marry Dionora?"

To marry the only woman he'd ever loved? Fate was never that kind to him. He lifted another shot—the first he knew of many—and toasted, "Here is to her rejecting me."

CHAPTER 6

"We're here." Hours had passed, and Stephan's arm wrapped Alexander's hip as he helped him up the short flight of stairs to the hotel entrance. Thankfully, the rain had stopped, and the walk from the bar had been a short one.

Alexander gazed up at the sign above the double doors. "Are you sure this is the right hotel?"

"For the fifth time, I know where I'm going." Stephan opened the door and helped Alexander in. "How many Dionora Specials did you drink tonight?"

"I lost count." Alexander took a deep breath and looked around the lobby. The slight smile on his face told Stephan that his friend believed he was in the right place. At the very least, Alexander didn't turn and walk out. "Not to worry. I'm still awake and alert."

Awake and alert? Hell. If human, Alexander would be dead. Right now, he was only a handful of Dionora Specials away from passing out. "You're more smashed than that night in London a few years ago when you thought you saw Dionora in a taxi," Stephan said, struggling to maneuver his friend past the hotel lobby.

"No, I'm not." Alexander stood straighter. "For one thing, I remember what town we're in."

"Okay, big guy." Stephan got Alexander down the hallway and used his key card to open their corner room. "What town are we in?"

"The one where my sweet Dionora lives." Alexander took a deep breath and let it out with a smile covering his now lovestruck face. "I still love her, you know."

It had been a while since Alexander had even mentioned Dionora's name, let alone confessed his love for her. But it was no secret. They went through this confession several times a year, usually around the holidays, Dionora's birthday, and any time a woman who resembled Dionora hit on Alexander. Oddly enough, he never took those women to bed.

Stephan managed to get Alexander into the room but couldn't get him into the adjoining bedroom, so he dumped him on the couch in the suite. Alexander's drunken stupor was always the same. Unless he got some blood into him, he'd start to age and go through the stages of grief. Denial that he had been stupid enough to let her go, anger at himself for obeying his parents' wishes, bargaining and making deals that if Stephan could find her that he'd make everything all right, and then the horrible depression would set in. He'd suffer through that last step for at least a day. He never did seem to get to the acceptance stage.

"You need some blood, we have a big day tomorrow."

Stephan walked to the suite's side bedroom to collect some bagged blood when a knock sounded at the door.

"I'll get it." He closed the refrigerator and glanced at his watch. "It's three a.m. Who would be stupid enough to knock on the door of two hungry vampires?"

Turning, Stephan saw Alexander getting off the couch.

"Maybe it's Dionora," Alexander said, glancing back at Stephan as he reached the door first. He opened it and found Margo, who was out of breath but all smiles.

"Hello, handsome," she said in a breathy voice.

Alexander leaned against the door jam, his face showing his disappointment. "Hello."

Before Stephan could tell Margo that it was too late for guests, she was already across the threshold and a few steps into the room. "I see we're not alone."

"Margo," Stephan said, his tone firm and his head shaking. He placed his hand on the doorknob and opened the door wider. "I don't think it's a good idea for you to be here."

She placed a finger on Alexander's chest and allowed it to trace across his muscles as she walked past him. She sat on the armrest of the couch, crossed her legs, and aimed her bedroom eyes at Alexander. "The night is young. I know the bars have closed, at least the good ones have, but I thought we could order a nightcap." She glared at Stephan as she caught her breath. "A private nightcap just between Alexander and me."

"You look beautiful, Margo, and I appreciate the effort…" Alexander motioned for her to leave.

"You are exactly the type of vampire I've been looking for. Tall, dark hair…" She stood and approached Alexander. Placing one hand in his hair and the other on his crotch, she added, "Sexy as hell."

She leaned in for a kiss, and Alexander backed away, nearly stumbling.

Stephan had never seen him turn down a woman, least of all a purebred vampire who'd delivered herself to his hotel room. Seeing Dionora must have really messed with his friend's head and heart.

"I was just going to bed."

"Alexander, you read my mind." She removed her coat, revealing a red lace teddy. She turned and sauntered back to the couch where she laid her outer garment down, giving both vampires a good look at her bare bottom.

Alexander's expression didn't change. He didn't stare at her butt, he didn't move toward her...he didn't even raise an eyebrow. It was so unlike his friend's usual norm when it came to women. If it had been him, Stephan would have already closed the door and had the teddy off the woman.

But, she wasn't there for him.

"How did you find us?" Stephan collected the coat and handed it back to her.

"I had to compel ten concierge desk captains across the city at the nicest hotels to text me if they saw Alexander." She took a deep breath. "I was several blocks away when I got the text that you were here."

Quite the hike in her four-inch heels.

Slutty, pushy, and excessively eager. Even drunk, Stephan knew Alexander never saw those things as virtues. Although, for a night of fun, that could be a different story.

But a wham-bam type of night usually meant more willingness from one's partner. Stephan didn't detect any heightened excitement from Margo. She was attracted to

Alexander, there was no doubt about that, but there was no strong smell of arousal coming from her, no sexual tension either. It could be because she had just run a mini–marathon in heels and had otherwise exerted herself, but Stephan suspected she was only here to land a husband, and any rich vampire would do.

"One moment, Margo." Alexander motioned with a head nod for Stephan to step into the bedroom. Once there, he said in a stern but soft voice, "I'm going to bed." An expression crept over his face that was deadly serious. "I only want Dionora, so fake Margo is yours if you want her." With that, he ushered Stephan out of the room and closed the bedroom door.

It wasn't the first time Alexander had passed on a woman, and not the first time he'd thought Stephan might enjoy the company instead. But the look on his face just now told Stephan that today was a turning point.

But he wasn't sure if that was good or bad. If Alexander chose Dionora, she could reject him and crush his heart. He needed Alexander to see Dionora again, without Margo, and try to win her back. They needed to arrive at the office early tomorrow before Margo showed up.

"I'm afraid he's turned in for the night." Stephan walked back to her and shook his head as if to say there was no use in her trying to change his mind. "I will have Alexander at your office at nine a.m. on the dot," he said, knowing that they opened at eight and hoping Dionora would be early.

Margo stared at the closed bedroom door, the expression on her face changing from wanton to horrified. "Was it something I said?"

She was beautiful and available and eager. The type of woman who easily fell into the bed of a second–choice man with a shoulder to cry on. It wouldn't take long to get her juices flowing, but Stephan doubted she would leave anytime soon. The last thing he wanted was to have Margo stay for breakfast and have another shot at convincing Alexander to choose her. It would also be bad if Dionora saw Margo arriving at the office tomorrow with them.

Plus, Alexander needed to drink some blood tonight to help his liver process all the alcohol. Stephan could use some blood as well, or he would age by tomorrow.

He helped Margo on with her coat. "We have a long day ahead of us, so you probably should leave."

Worry laced her eyes, and Stephan knew she'd probably worry about her chances at a proposal until tomorrow. "Tell you what," he said, "Alexander loves sheer clothing. Wear your sexiest, see–through outfit tomorrow, and remind him what he passed on tonight."

A light twinkle of hope shone in her eyes. "Do you think that will work?"

A slutty outfit on her would remind Alexander of what had happened tonight, and it would definitely make him not want to pick her. "Let's hope so," he lied, getting her out of the room and locking the door behind her.

Stephan collected two bags of blood from the refrigerator and knocked on the bedroom door before entering.

"No woman will ever compare to Dionora. My life is ruined," Alexander said with a low moan, his arm resting across his eyes as he lay on the bed in the dark room.

Shit. They were already at the depression stage.

CHAPTER 7

"I'm very busy, Edmund." Dionora sat back down at her desk and typed away on the keyboard, her nails clicking as she worked in the dim room. "I don't have a lot of time before my first client arrives." She yawned and looked at the clock. The office would open in half an hour.

"You didn't come home last night." Edmund stood in Dionora's office, his wife, Sarah, by his side. A worried look crossed his face, one that Dionora had seen many times since he was the overprotective brother.

"What?" Dionora asked, grateful that it was too early for the Council employees to be in the office. It wasn't as if she were throwing a party, but she shouldn't be entertaining her family members while at work.

"You look younger today, and you got a manicure," Sarah said, interrupting and grabbing Dionora's hand, which caused Dionora to stop typing. Sarah looked questioningly at her husband in a here's–the–proof sort of way.

Knowing she'd get nothing done until she found out what they wanted, Dionora took a deep breath and leaned more into her chair. "What's going on?"

"Have you been here all night?" Edmund asked.

Dionora had gone home to get a change of clothes and then she ran into the market for a mani–pedi with a stop at a beauty boutique for a makeover. "Pretty much. I have a big case to work on. Why are you asking?"

"So, you haven't seen him yet." Edmund glanced over at Sarah, some secret passing silently between them.

Dionora didn't have time for games. "Spill it, or leave. I'm busy."

"That bastard, Alexander, was in our bar last night." Edmund's jaw tightened, and his hands balled into fists. "He ordered drinks and didn't recognize me."

Sarah nodded her head. "I served them a ton of shots last night. It was only when the blond one showed up that they recognized Edmund."

"It was that weasel, Stephan," Edmund said. "That's when I left and had Sarah spy on them since they don't know her."

Fate hated her. Dionora wanted to tell her family about her great triumph of screwing Alexander over. Or, at the very least, rejecting him when all was said and done. Now, two members of her family knew of her plan, with chances of them *all* knowing. "Alexander was drinking?" she asked nonchalantly as she checked her phone for messages from her parents. There were no texts, so they must not have been told the news.

Edmund's face turned stoic. "So you knew he was in Paris?"

"He was drinking heavily last night?" she repeated the question.

"Straight vodka," Edmund said. "So much, in fact, that I have to order more for tonight."

Guzzling down drinks seemed so unlike the old Alexander Dionora had known. She motioned to the chairs by her desk so her family could take the seats and she could fill them in. "He came to my office to find a wife."

"The nerve of that bastard." Edmund's fist hit her desk. His face reddened, and his fangs extended. She loved how predatory he became when it came to her, but she wasn't a young little girl anymore. She could fight—and win against—the big boys now.

"Don't worry. He's hoping to find a bride, and I gave him a horror show of a list to pick from. I'm positive he'll reject everyone…" She thought for a moment. "Except for one. And I can't get her off the damn list."

"The bar was busy last night, but every time I was near their table, they mentioned something about a rejection." Sarah's eyes narrowed. "I overheard something about them hoping the *woman* he chooses will reject him so he can get the ten-year penalty."

"What?" That can't be right. Dionora felt trapped in a corner with no way to escape. She had made that list with the sole purpose of him rejecting it flat-out. Why would he want a ten-year penalty?

Hell, why would he even approach the Verheirates Schlange if he didn't want a bride? None of it made sense.

"Alexander wants the rejection to come from the woman. Not him." Sarah gave Dionora a half-hearted shrug. "The bar was very crowded and noisy, but I'm positive that's what the two of them were talking about."

"So, let me get this straight..." Dionora's mind raced with different scenarios, and she had to get things clear in her head. "He wants to choose a woman from his list and be rejected by her?"

"We think so," Edmund said.

Mentally going through the candidates one by one, Dionora realized that all of the women would jump at the chance to marry him—the only exception being her.

So, either he'd marry a woman he had nothing in common with, or he'd choose her.

Her mind did a mental happy–dance. He would pick her. She was the only option. He would choose her, and she'd get to reject him.

An evil smile, nice and sinister, spread across her lips until she realized what she had done. If what her brother said were true, then she was now giving Alexander exactly what he wanted.

Damn.

But she couldn't worry about that. She wanted revenge, plain and simple.

Dionora glanced at the outer office and, still, no one was around. Dionora filled Edmund and Sarah in on the other five women on Alexander's list, careful not to mention any names but her own and Margo's. She went through Plan A and Plan B with them and even added a Plan C where he chose Margo.

"I love it." Sarah smiled. "And Margo's been so mean to you, if he chooses Plan C, she'll be out of your hair."

"I bet he'll go with Plan B and choose you." Edmund's eyes twinkled with the wide smile he now wore. "Can we stay and watch you reject him?" Edmund pulled out his phone. "I can take a video if you want."

"The selection process is private. If a video leaked out, I'd be fired for sure."

Noise came from the outer office space; employees coming in. Dionora knew she had to put on a more professional air. "You shouldn't be here." She stood to lead them out of her office.

"Tell us all about it when you get home tonight," Edmund whispered while Sarah giggled.

CHAPTER 8

*D*ionora's coworkers filed into work and she stood outside her office, her body taut with anticipation. Alexander and Stephan had shown up a few minutes ago and were in her office talking while she gathered some paperwork and waited for Margo to arrive.

She also needed some time to think.

Unfortunately, she couldn't hear a bloody word through the thick, wooden door. She would have given anything to listen to her dear ex–love squirm under the pressure of having to make a selection from what she figured was possibly the worst bridal list ever.

She had hoped that he'd simply reject the list outright and say goodbye to another mating for at least ten years. But now, thanks to Sarah's eavesdropping, she hoped that he would pick the alligator lady and move to Florida.

So long, happiness. So long, wedded bliss. So long, Alexander.

God, she was good. It had taken a thorough database search to find those women, but what a jackpot of a discovery they were. A slight giggle leaked out and caught the attention of the receptionist, but Dionora quickly recovered with a throat clearing and scratch of the head as if waiting impatiently for her client's decision.

She paced on her new stiletto heels, which she had bought a while ago, but had had no occasion to wear. That was, until today. Her dress was a classy knockoff, her makeup was from a counter girl at the local shop this morning, and her hair was... Well, it looked really nice. Spending an extra thirty minutes to blow it out really did make her hairstyle pop and have people take notice. She'd have to remember to do that more often.

She stared at the door, knowing that Plan A would not happen. It didn't take long to scream an obscenity about a list, or laugh about it and then reject it. Sarah was right. They must be choosing someone to be his bride.

Plan C was underway, and she knew they were discussing Margo. They had to be.

Plastic–personality Margo.

Alexander would pick her, and then Margo would be off to Venice for her wedding and their miserable marriage. Since Dionora and Margo held the same office title, that would leave Dionora as the team lead for the selection process—and she had only worked here a few weeks.

Hopefully, there'd be a promotion and more money for that role.

She looked at the clock on the wall. It was five minutes until eight in the morning. Margo would likely be here soon. Of course, she wouldn't realize that Alexander and Stephan had shown up a good ten minutes ago.

Dionora went to a cabinet and grabbed a rejection

notice. Just in case Alexander picked her, she wanted that document handy to throw in his face. She had the time, so she filled it out.

Name. Address. Sexual orientation? Hmmm, that was different from the forms she had filled out the last time. Of course, she had completed the acceptance forms then.

"Reason for rejection." She was tempted to write *heartless bastard*, or list him as *impotent* since this was an official form that would carry over to any future marital pairing. Dionora even noticed a box to check if the person was presented as a virgin and wasn't.

God, they needed to change these forms. The exact wording was:*female isn't a virgin*. Nobody cared if the man was a whoring bastard. Alexander had rejected her the last time due to this little box. She had made love to Alexander during their courtship, and that was the knife he'd used to stab her in the back. It had gotten him out of the ten-year penalty and allowed him to marry his now ex-wife. It had also ruined Dionora's reputation and sullied her name with the Council.

She finally decided to write:*past experiences leading to irreconcilable differences*. The reason was vague enough, and she could supply more details later if needed.

The form didn't take long to fill out, and Dionora paced some more before Margo finally came in. Margo would make sure to enter their office first and try to control the rest of the meeting, probably making a last-ditch effort to sway the vote in her favor—which was presumably why her dress had a plunging neckline and a high-cut slit.

Margo hung her coat up on the rack in the corner of the room. Her hand smoothed away imaginary wrinkles in her dress as she readied herself to enter their office. The receptionist motioned toward the door and said something, which caused Margo's eyes to light up.

She now knew that Alexander was already here.

With vampire speed, Dionora grabbed the rejection document and beat Margo to their office door. She entered the room ahead of Margo, who closed the door behind her. Dionora's stride showed her confidence as she walked past Margo to her side of the desk and took a seat.

"All right, gentlemen," Margo said, making Dionora cringe at the offered title. "Have you decided whom to marry?"

Dionora's gaze traveled from Alexander to Stephan and back. Resting her gaze on Alexander, she waited for him to choose Margo.

Alexander held tightly to the folder in his hands. "It was quite the list." His gaze sought out Margo, and he gave her a slight nod. "With some...nice competition."

Margo's fake smile turned Dionora's stomach. With the light in the room coming in from the window, Dionora now noticed that the front of Margo's dress was see–through. Alexander had never liked overt gestures like that. Dionora now gripped the rejection paper under the desk, feeling that Plan B was going to happen and that he would say her name.

His soft green eyes locked onto hers. It seemed as if he stared at Dionora for several minutes, but she refused to blink. She wasn't going to turn this into a staring competition or a war.

She twisted the rejection paperwork under her desk, not realizing how badly she wanted to throw it in his face.

"I choose you, Dionora." His voice sounded commanding and decisive in her tiny office.

Her heart rate quickened. She had known Plan B was a possibility, but she needed a minute to regroup and to uncrumple the paperwork in her hands.

"You choose me?" she asked in a high–pitched squeak, not realizing how tense her body had gotten.

"You."

All eyes turned to her, and she felt as if the air had gotten sucked out of the room. She couldn't breathe.

She gazed over at Margo, who stared at her with mere slits for eyes, her lips thinned to a slash. There'd be hell to pay later once Dionora rejected the betrothal and continued working in this office, but she didn't care. She had a life to ruin. "Margo, can you please give us a minute?"

The woman left the room, and Dionora felt a little sorry for her. Margo had wanted to land a wealthy man, like many vampire women did. There was no crime in that, but it wouldn't be Alexander. At least, not today.

"I think we may be able to work it out this time." Alexander waved dismissively at Stephan like any master would to their servant and best friend who needed them to handle all the details. "We can fly to Venice tonight and have my parents' blessing by the morning."

She suspected that his sly smile held a lie. She hadn't been his daily gal–pal in a long time, but she knew Alexander Marino. At least, she had back in the day.

A fake smile spread across her lips, one that was both reassuring and sinful. "I see." She straightened her dress and sat straight, her back leaning into her creaky chair. Her hand curled around the rejection paperwork.

The two men stared at her, their eyes glued to her every move. Silence filled the room, and she could hear the ticking of the clock on the wall.

With her legs crossed, her right foot began to tremble under the table. A bad nervous habit that she had thought was long gone, now back to torment her.

She placed her hand on her knee and took a deep breath. This was her moment, and she was going to savor it.

She stared deeply into Alexander's eyes. The green, puppy–dog eyes that she had lost herself in so many times in her youth. Just as she was about to throw the paper-work at him, she remembered what Sarah had said. That he wanted to get a rejection and the ten–year penalty.

Her heart raced. She didn't know what game he was playing, but the last thing she wanted was to give Alexander what he desired. Her brother and sister–in–law probably did overhear him correctly in the bar the other night.

But to have the chance to reject him. Her heart was torn.

She should have thought this through. If she rejected Alexander, he'd get his way. If she *didn't* reject him, her Christmas plans with her family were possibly gone, and she may have to spend the holiday with the one man she hated more than anything else. Or worse, she might actually get married to the bastard.

Oh, hell no.

She could reject him a moment before the wedding took place. There would be no penalty if she canceled due to just cause. She just needed a valid reason, with proof.

Anger bubbled up. She couldn't cancel the wedding

because he wasn't a virgin. That was a double–standard that needed to be fixed.

She could claim that he had feelings for another. An eyebrow perked up. Maybe that was why he needed a rejection from his chosen bride?

That made sense. He wanted to enter a marriage of love, and his parents insisted that he go through a Council–arranged one. Getting a rejection would allow him to marry the woman of his choice. Dionora just had to figure out who it was, reject him publicly at the last minute, and then...shit, without proof, she'd get penalized, and Alexander would still get his way.

Damn it.

Stephan leaned in, waiting for her answer. The dutiful sidekick who was always at Alexander's side. Maybe she could say that Alexander had romantic interests in Stephan? Some sort of underlying, homosexual urges that he wasn't able to contain anymore and that Stephan was the one Alexander had feelings for. Then she'd be able to throw Stephan under the bus at the last moment, too.

Not that doing so would be fair to either of them.

Plus, she needed proof.

"My dear?" Alexander said in his sexy voice that she used to love, but which now made her skin crawl. "I need an answer."

The mischievous smile told her that he wasn't being completely honest and that he wanted something. Dionora hated that smile. She wanted to smack it off his face.

His eyebrow rose. "My dear?"

Her mind raced.

She glanced at Stephan, whose grin seemed as fake as

Alexander's with one exception. He looked like he needed a certain outcome to make him happy.

Good Lord, she wanted to get them both with one fell swoop, to teach them both a lesson.

Alexander wanted the rejection. In her heart, she knew that Stephan wanted whatever Alexander wanted. He was a lap dog like that.

If Dionora were clever enough, she could get her revenge in before Christmas and still have time with her family during the holiday.

She could have Alexander wine and dine her, jump through some hoops to please her, and maybe she could torture him a bit before she rejected him. From her time with the Verheirates Schlange, she had learned one thing:brides were allowed Bridal Demands. Many of them. In the short time she had worked here, she had seen some doozies.

A halfway, not–quite–so–decent plan was forming in her head, and she knew exactly what to do.

"Accepted." Her determined voice, short and curt, cut through the silence of the room. She placed her hand on her knee to keep it from dancing around under the desk.

Alexander's jaw fell open, just like she had hoped. Stephan actually looked happy, the sniveling weasel.

"Wonderful,"Alexander said through pursed lips. "We'll leave tonight."

She leaned forward and narrowed her eyes at him, coming up with the first Bridal Demand she'd make. He always enjoyed being in control, but now he'd have to adhere to *her* schedule. "Actually, I can't leave." Her hands waved, indicating her office. "I do have a job."

"The Verheirates Schlange selection should give you some time off, right?" Stephan asked.

Stephan. An old childhood friend, a boy much like a brother to her back in the day, and a rotten friend in the end. Breakups were always hard, and friends always picked sides, but she had lost that jerk in the process of having her heart broken. He and Alexander had always been tight, and the fact that Stephan was here now irked her even more.

She gave him a stern glance. Of course, the selection would supersede any work schedule, but she still had some cards to play. "My family is very *conventional*, as I'm sure you both remember." She paused for effect to allow that to sink in, but she doubted they took the hint. "They'll have a list of Bridal Demands."

"Demands?" Alexander's eyebrow shot up.

"Bridal Demands, yes. It's tradition." She felt herself gloating and toned down her smile so she wouldn't give anything away. "I can draft up the agreement today and have it sent to your hotel tonight. The engagement can begin in a few days' time, once the weekend starts and I can get a replacement for myself here at the office."

"That's fine." Alexander nodded. "You can fly to Venice when you're ready."

"Not just that," she said with a wickedness in her voice that surprised even her. "As your consort pro–temp, according to the traditional rules of an arranged marriage, I am to be chaperoned and protected on any travels to visit future family."

"Hell, we can spend a few days in Paris," Stephan said, glancing at Alexander, whose hardened expression narrowed in on Dionora.

"You may need a few days, maybe a week here in Paris." She settled into the chair, enjoying the power play. "There is a list of marriage requirements that the bride's family may request. Some may seem archaic, but to my old-fashioned family, they find them charming."

"Gisele and Ricold? Old fashioned?" Alexander sputtered, clearly remembering how formal her upbringing had been.

"My family is local, which is convenient," she said, ignoring his remark.

"Convenient for what?" Stephan asked in a worried tone.

"I'll get a list to you by tonight of my family's courtship requirements. We'll make sure to satisfy those needs before heading off to see... I'm sorry, what are your parents' names again, Alexander?"

His brow lifted and slid into his hairline. "It's in my file."

"I'll look it up, then," she said, knowing full well what their names were.

Not quite ready to let them off the hook, she added more. "Plus, I hate to fly. We'll have to travel by train when we go see your parents. And," she said, leaning in and squaring off with Alexander, "you are not to tell them that I am your chosen one."

Alexander's lips curled upward, and his smile looked tantalizing and pure evil. "My parents hate surprises, so agreed."

"We're traveling by train?" Stephan's gaze ping-ponged between the two. Whether he had a complaint to file, the air filled with contention, and he decided to say, "I can make the arrangements."

Alexander stared at Dionora, hard and stern to the point where she wasn't sure she wouldn't crack under the pressure. "When should we leave for Italy, my dear."

She flashed one last wicked smile before standing up and ushering them to the door. "I should be presented to your parents the night of the new moon. So, about a week."

"New moon." Stephan chuckled. When the silence lay thickly between them, he added, "That's good timing. I'll get us tickets and take care of everything."

"Please leave your contact information with the receptionist before you leave. I'll have a courier send over the marriage documents tonight."

CHAPTER 9

"We should have read the report last night," Stephan said as he and Alexander entered the Cistern and Fox Pub on Rue de Chien street, a different bar than the night before so they wouldn't run into Edmund. "The sooner we get everything finalized, the better."

"Everything finalized?" Alexander turned to face Stephan and lifted an eyebrow questioningly. "Have you already read the report?"

"I glanced at it." He held up the folder. "The list of requirements goes on for fifteen pages."

Alexander noticed that they stood in front of the bar stools, not casting clear reflections in the mirror. He continued walking. "We have several days in Paris. Nothing has to be done on Dionora's schedule." He led his friend to a back booth and took a seat. "Besides, it's Paris. When was the last time we were here?"

"It's been a good thirty years." Stephan removed his thick winter coat and set it on the booth next to him.

Neither he nor Alexander needed the outer garments for warmth, but they did help them blend in. As Alexander took off his coat, Stephan grabbed a napkin from the dispenser and wiped the spills away from the tabletop. He then put the marriage documentation on the flat surface.

"I understand there are originally eighty–three traditional Bridal Demands. Dionora has only marked about twenty of them that her family wants done."

"Twenty?" Alexander asked.

"Consider yourself lucky." Stephan glanced at the list, his face pinching with the things he now read. "Okay, some are not too bad. At least, I doubt they will take days to complete."

"Days?" Days of being near the one that got away? Alexander took in a deep breath and smelled the freshly cut lemons and limes from behind the bar. He knew that his shot for happiness with Dionora was long gone. But, if there were ever a time to get to know her again…to relearn the curves of her body, the arching of her back as he brought her to orgasm…

"Chastity and honor are highly regarded virtues on this list, so wipe that smile off your face."

Alexander rolled his eyes. "So, no fun and games?"

"Hey, it's up to the bride's discretion, and, according to this, there is to be no carnal knowledge of each other before nuptials."

"Carnal knowledge," Alexander scoffed, almost to the point of a slight chuckle, "are you reading that verbatim?"

"Carnal knowledge and nuptials." Stephan pointed to the words on the document. "They are the exact words that are written down."

"Bloody hell." Alexander didn't want to jump through

hoops. He didn't want to disappoint Dionora. He just wanted a quick rejection. "I want her rejection of me done in days. It's already been dragging on long enough."

It had been bad enough being put through the process of a bridal selection again, but to have Dionora back on his list? Alexander would gladly accept her as a bride. But to know the marriage would be rejected, if not by her parents than by his? He hadn't wanted to read the marriage report last night, nor even today. All he could think about was happier times and how much he had hurt her. The sooner this was all behind him, the better.

A waitress came by for their orders. Before another Dionora Special could be placed, Stephan ordered some coffees and then dismissed the woman.

"I'm not in the mood for coffee," Alexander said, his dismissive tone falling on deaf ears. He stared at his friend, who was busy reading the report.

"By the way, did you fuck Margie?"

"Margo. And, no." Stephan didn't even glance up. "I'm surprised you even remember last night."

Alexander remembered the drinking, the bar–hopping, and even how desperate the blonde had been to land him as a husband. She couldn't compare to how wonderful Dionora would be as a wife, but then, he wasn't going to marry either of them.

Margo was a one–night type of woman. It was a shame. Even though he didn't want her, someone should have slept with her.

Stephan was engrossed in the report, so Alexander had to ask, "What is our first step?"

"You have to be formally introduced to Dionora,"

Stephan read from the list. His fingers doing air quotes around the word *formally*.

The Bridal Demands were already sounding stupid. "Introduced? I've known her my whole life."

"It's a formality, but something you have to take seriously." Stephan continued reading the document. "Someone not of your family line, someone with prestige and honor, must acquaint the two of you."

"Fine, that's you, then. Introduce us."

"Prestige and honor." Stephan touched his chest. "Thanks, man."

"You're the only other one here, so continue."

If Stephan felt insulted, he didn't show it. He merely said, "It may seem silly, or even trivial, but you must give her your card."

"My card?" He rolled his eyes and gave a slight cringe. "I didn't even use a calling card when they were customary."

The waitress arrived and set down their coffees, placing them on paper coasters. The two men waited until she walked out of earshot before continuing.

"You give her your card, and then she will, and I quote, 'notify the lucky gentleman by giving him her card in return if interested.'"

Alexander grabbed a napkin from the table. "I need to find a pen, then."

"Hey." Stephan grabbed the paper from Alexander's hand. "You rejected this girl and treated her like used dental floss. You can get her a real card."

"But I…"

"No." Stephan's voice sounded defiant in a way that

Alexander wasn't familiar with. "You're going to follow each of these demands."

Alexander didn't typically back down, but he wanted to make sure that Dionora was the one who rejected him —so he was willing to play her game. "Where the hell am I going to find a stationery store to make me one fucking card?"

Stephan nodded to the document. "She has an address here."

He wondered how many little side trips she had planned for them. "She is either taking this very seriously, or not seriously at all."

"I vote you take her family seriously."

Or… "Why can't I act like an ass and be rejected by them?"

"You can't. Not according to your parents. Dionora and her parents can only reject you if they are unsatisfied with your ability to meet all their requirements. You have to complete the tasks. You said your parents are not playing around this time."

Alexander knew it was true. "Fine. After drinks, we'll find that stationery shop. What's next?"

"You then must ask permission from her parents to call on her for a chaperoned visit. That will allow you to impress the parents and you will be allowed to call on her again."

"Her parents hate me."

"They agreed to the courtship, so don't be an ass." Stephan read further on the list. "We need to order a bottle of metheglin."

"What the devil is metheglin?"

"It's just honey mead. Any brand will do. According to

custom, as the moon goes through all its phases, the betrothed couple drinks it. Honey mead is made with honey. Obviously. Hence where we get the word:*honeymoon*."

"Mead will taste like ass unless there is blood in it."

"Then alter the recipe," Stephan said, just as the waitress approached their table with refills on their coffees. After asking the waitress for the mead, and waiting for her to be out of hearing range, Stephan added, "Dionora said her family is willing to allow the honeymoon ale for just the duration of the new moon." His friend's gaze now rested on Alexander. "You only have to do it for a few days until the moon is full, not for the required month."

"That's good to know."

"Is she big on poetry?"

"Now that is just about enough..." With a look from Stephan that told him not to question the requirements, he answered, "I don't believe she ever enjoyed poetry."

"I don't remember her liking it either. But we need to buy a poetry book." He shook his head. "And some flowers."

"Seems like she gets a lot with the groom's family getting nothing."

"Oh, there is a dowry," Stephan said. "Once a husband is found, the father of the bride pays the groom's family a dowry in exchange for his daughter's hand in marriage. In case of the bride's family being lower-class, the dowry might be a farm animal," Stephan said, reading from the document.

"Great. A cow for my family to milk in the morning."

Stephan read ahead in the list, a slight chuckle escaping his throat, telling Alexander that more games were afoot. "Oh, there is more. But we'll deal with each one as it comes."

"And then either her family will reject me, or we can go to Venice for my parents' rejection?"

Stephan lifted his finger and caught Alexander's full attention. "If we do get to Venice with her, you cannot tell them you're bringing home Dionora. She is to be presented to them as a surprise." He made a waving motion with his hands. "Unveiled to them, so to speak." He glanced at the document. "Oh, my bad. We need to actually buy her a silk veil." He squinted his eyes and read, "With embroidered purple violets."

Stephan glanced up. "That's rather specific."

Alexander rolled his eyes. If Dionora needed all these details, then he'd play along.

"Your parents can reject her at the formal meeting, which is to be a ball in her honor, whether or not the marriage is to proceed."

"Great. My mother can throw a huge party for…"—he paused before saying *"the girl of my dreams,"*—for Dionora before crushing her spirit once again. Maybe there'll be time for her family to add it to their Christmas letter."

CHAPTER 10

"These are the nicest ones I have," Dionora's mother, Gisele, said as she lay a beautiful dress on the bed, its red lace catching on the sequins of the dress now beneath it. "I have some nice shoes to match." Her fingers straightened the outfits to smooth out any creases.

Dionora crossed the room, her torn dressing gown—tied with a thin sash around her waist—showing her bare legs and fancy underclothes. "I don't go much in for frills." Her finger traced the lace bodice of the garment. "These are so nice."

Dionora looked lovingly at her mother. "Thanks for suggesting that I move back home and take this new job."

"You're lucky your mother had these old dresses, although they seem a bit too fancy for work," her father, Ricold, said as he eyed the clothing. "So, tell us, what's the exciting news? A promotion?" he said, a proud smile showing his joy.

"I just started working there. It's no promotion."

Dionora gave the clothes a last cursory look. "Everything comes back in style eventually." She smiled approvingly at the color of the dress on top. "Red was always his favorite. The color of questionable women back in the day."

"A man?" Ricold asked, his voice sounding hopeful.

A grin—wide and fangy—spread across Gisele's lips. "Of course, a man!" She beamed her smile to her daughter. "Did you meet someone new? Or have you had your eye on someone?"

Ricold asked, "Is he why you moved back to France?"

Her parents' giddiness didn't surprise Dionora, they had always wanted true happiness and love for their daughter—especially since her experiences with men didn't usually turn out so well. But they were always hopeful. Dionora pushed the outfits aside and gestured for her mom and dad to sit on the bed. "Someone from my past."

"Someone from your past?" Gisele repeated as she joined her daughter on the bed.

"Is this why Edmund and Sarah told your mother that we needed to talk to you?" Ricold glanced at Gisele. "Did they talk to you about anything?"

Gisele shook her head no.

When the two sat and stared at her, wonderment and love in their eyes, Dionora added, "Do you remember Alexander Marino?"

Ricold stood, his body stiff. "No." He turned his back and took a step, but then seemed to swirl with anger and spun to glare at Dionora. "We're not going through this again."

"That beast," Gisele exclaimed, her hand touching her chest as if her heart panged for her daughter. "Is he here in Paris?" She pointed to her daughter's youthful appearance. "That's why you lowered your age to your twenties again. To impress him."

"Oh," Dionora said, the glint in her eyes and the smirk on her face lifting her lips to show the tips of her fangs. "I'm not trying to impress him. I'm trying to torture him."

Ricold sat back on the bed. "I like that idea."

"Ricold," Gisele chided, a questioning look in her eye.

Dionora's father smiled. "Go on."

"He's looking for a mate through my office, and he brought Stephan with him." Dionora giggled as she explained the four vampire women she had chosen for Alexander. "I'm glad that I was able to choose the list, but then my officemate, Margo, added her name."

Her mother's eyebrow lifted. "Is that the same Margo who's been giving you a hard time?"

"Yes. She's been a bit of a hard–ass, but she has taught me a lot about the job."

"Then she can have that miserable Alexander and deal with his family." Ricold's hand raked through his hair, and Dionora could see the worry lines forming around his eyes.

"I made sure to fill the list with losers."

"You're playing with fire, my dear," Gisele warned, her tone motherly and smooth, but with a slight lilt in her voice that told Dionora that her mother enjoyed the selection list just as much as she did.

In a softened tone, Dionora added, "I also put my name on his list."

A gasp escaped Gisele's throat. "You know you endangered your chances of being on someone else's selection later. You do realize that, don't you?"

"It's fine." Dionora didn't care. A chance to mess with Alexander? She'd take that any day of the week.

"He'll have a month to decide," Ricold said. "So make sure he doesn't choose you." Her father waved a hand toward the dresses now piled on the edge of the bed. "All of this won't impress that bastard or his family."

"His family expedited the paperwork, so he only had a day to choose." She glanced at her parents but didn't make eye contact. "He chose me."

A gurgling sound echoed from the back of her father's throat. "I never thought I'd see that man again, and here you are, asking us to allow him to marry you." He shook his head, his expression determined. "The answer is a definite no."

"Absolutely not." Gisele's face, creased with worry, told Dionora that the two did not understand her plans. "We're not going to give our consent. Not after the way that vamp's family treated us."

Gisele sat straighter on the bed and shot a questioning stare at her daughter. "I'm surprised Alexander didn't refuse you right then and there and leave the office."

"I have no plans to..." Dionora paused for a moment and chose her words carefully. "To be mated to a fiend such as him."

"Then why go to the trouble of...?" Ricold asked.

No, her father didn't understand. A scorned woman, no matter how long ago the burn had occurred, was always someone to be reckoned with. For a vampire who had secured his mate early in life and who enjoyed the comforts of a perfect companion, her father had never had to experience a bitch wreaking havoc upon him. But then again, her dad was a saint who only deserved the best.

"Daddy, a girl must have her fun." Dionora'seyes narrowed devilishly. "They'll stay two more days in Paris until the new moon. Then, I'll go with Alexander to Venice. I plan to dump him in front of his parents during the huge ball they're throwing in my honor."

Gisele snickered. "You're giving Isabella only a few days to plan a ball?" She took a deep breath, her eyes showing her approval. "She must be scrambling to get everything done and compelling every human within earshot to do her bidding."

"Unless they reject you again." The creases in her father's face deepened around his forehead and eyes, the way they always did when he showed concern for her.

"There is to be no rejection ahead of time. Part of the deal was that he couldn't tell his parents whom he was bringing home. I am to be a surprise."

A wide grin spread across Gisele's face. "I'd love to be there."

"This deal is between you and that weasel, Alexander. Is Stephan telling those bastards anything?" Ricold asked.

"Doubtful. The Marinos were never his favorite growing up either." She crossed the room and gave her father a reassuring pat on the shoulder. "Plus, I've made arrangements. Let's just say Stephan will be running all over town the next few days to make me happy. Both will come calling this weekend."

"I won't let the bastards through the door," Ricold said, shaking his head. "They're not welcome in my home."

"Hear her out, dear," Gisele said firmly. "I'm enjoying the idea of a little payback."

"Thanks, Mom." Dionora's gaze darted to her father. "And, you'll have a gift for him when he comes." When her parents glared at her, she countered, "I'll have your roles in this little play all worked out by tomorrow morning. It will require some creative drink–making on your part, Mother, and some interesting purchases on yours, Father…but we'll have Alexander either running from this house in shame, or so frustrated that he'll be half the man that he thinks he is."

"If I don't beat him up the second he comes to the door."

"Daddy!"

Ricold stared at the ceiling, then let out a deep breath and seemingly tried to relax. "For the chance to torture the poor sod, I suppose I can entertain the men in my home," he said, his voice deflated, but his tone sounding as if he were coming around to the idea.

"Plus, I can get back at Stephan for no longer being my friend and treating me like the enemy. That is a nice bonus."

"That shrill–voiced little pipsqueak isn't nearly as guilty as Alexander. But good for you, dear," Gisele exclaimed.

Dionora picked up the bagged blood from the night-stand. "I appreciate you letting me stay with you while I settle into my new job. I'm sorry to throw this on you during the holidays, but when Alexander and Stephan walked into the office yesterday… I couldn't resist."

Her mother's smile, crafty and spirited, told Dionora that, even if the plan were risky, she too appreciated the game. "If it makes you happy, we're happy to do whatever you want."

"Within reason. We'll even reject the marriage contract outright if you want."

"No," Dionora said, a spark in her eye. "I'm the one that will do the rejecting this time. I want to do it and see the look in their eyes."

"That's a good plan, dear," her mother said.

Ricold pointed to the bagged blood, the red cross sticker with A+ on the front. "Extra blood?"

Letting out a sigh, she said, "I have to lose a few more years. The Council insists that all brides be at their base age." She picked up the bag and the goblet that rested next to it. "I'll be back to my Jahrling age of twenty–two for the rest of the week until Alexander is shamed at the ball."

"I'm surprised his family is still in Italy," Ricold said.

"Established, well–off, and desperate for him to settle down. They expedited his paperwork through my office. That's how I know he's ripe for revenge."

Her father stood and pointed a shaking finger in Dionora's direction. "You be careful," he said, enunciating each word.

"And let us know what you need us to do," Gisele said, leaning in and kissing Dionora goodnight. "We'll let you eat and…" She pointed to the blood. "Do what you need to do."

Dionora watched as her parents left, turning off the light so only the dim light of the nightstand lit up the room. She then poured the bagged blood into the goblet and stared at the crimson delight. "Cheers," she uttered before she took the first sip.

The blood, slightly warmed from a water bottle it had rested on, coated her tongue and slid down her parched throat. The type A+ was always her favorite. Something savored and enjoyed whenever she could get it from her local blood supplier. Now, as a potential bride to a wealthy family, she could order as much as she liked.

And she planned to stockpile it. Just another perk of being the future ex–wife of Alexander Marino.

She sipped the blood but knew full well that she'd be undergoing bloodlust soon with the amount she needed to ingest. Fully sated vampires, their bodies knowing that blood was available, turned to mating. And, being at her Jahrling age meant that she'd be fertile.

Not that Alexander would lay a hand on her.

She leaned back on the bed and waited for her spleen to process the blood from her digestive tract to her circulatory one. The burning of her eyes and the extension of her fangs had her catching her breath. Her racing heart and mind turned towards thoughts of Alexander—not that she had intended to focus her attention on him. His Playboy smirk, and his body that had always been...scrumptious.

CHAPTER 11

"*W*ake up," Stephan shouted from the outer room, rousing Alexander from a less–than–peaceful sleep.

Alexander turned into the pillow, his extended fang grazing the silk cover. "Go away."

"I called ahead and arranged breakfast." Stephan plodded into the bedroom of the hotel suite and opened the window coverings. "Get up."

Waving his arm around him, Alexander muttered, "Toss her onto the bed. I'll bite her in a minute."

"Are you still drunk from last night?" Stephan hit him squarely in the arm, forcing Alexander to sit up and look around. "We didn't have company last night." He then gazed sternly at his friend. "And we have none this morning. Or have you forgotten that you are a promised man?"

Forgotten? How could he forget? He had spent the entire night tossing and turning with evocative dreams that had featured only Dionora. Her smile, her sleek body... He had thought he'd forgotten all about her.

Forgotten about her playfulness, her spirit, and the unique way she could always get under his skin. The only woman to ever really know him.

"You kept moaning Dionora's name last night. I thought you swore those days were long gone."

Shit. Of course, Stephan had heard him. Leaving Dionora practically at the altar all those years ago had not been his idea, but rather a decree from his parents. Living without her...well, if Stephan hadn't been there all those years ago, Alexander wasn't sure how he would have survived.

"Those days *are* long gone." Dionora and her parents would see to that unless his parents worked their magic again.

"I'm just saying." Stephan let out a deep sigh and then shook his head. "You don't still have feelings for her, do you?" With worry in his eyes, he added, "I mean, this is Dionora."

A nervous laugh escaped before Alexander could catch it, and before Stephan could possibly pick up on any raw feelings that still lingered. "You said something about breakfast?"

"Shower." Stephan stood and made his way to the bedroom door. "I'm going to pick up some fresh flowers at the market."

Alexander watched as his best friend left, closing the door with a stern don't–go–back–to–bed glare before heading out. He wondered if Stephan would remember that Dionora liked roses.

~

After getting ready, Alexander followed Stephan down the streets of Paris, careful to stay on the tree–lined sidewalks for shade. They bumped into many people out enjoying a crisp morning walk and stopping near the colorful displays in the storefront windows filled with Christmas stuff.

They crossed the street and weaved around some parked cars toward more stores, which had green–striped awnings and bowls of icy water out for dogs. Alexander noticed that a flower shop sat among the stores, and he assumed that was where Stephan had bought the roses.

Alexander carried the bunch of long–stemmed roses in his hand—white, the color of pure love. Stephan had said it was all the market had, but after wandering the streets where the peddlers were situated, Alexander knew that was a lie. But then, he would have chosen white roses, as well. Splendid and sleek, with long stems to match Dionora's long, creamy–skinned legs.

The legs he had dreamed were around him all night last night. Not that such a thing would ever happen again in real life.

If he were going to break her heart, or at the very least piss her off for several more decades, then she at least deserved some nice flowers.

The walk, however long, felt like a blessing. It allowed Alexander time to think; allowed him to consider what he was doing. But it wasn't long enough to change his mind.

His parents needed to get off his back. He needed to move on. He needed to get back to his life. He hadn't been to South Africa yet, and that had always been on his bucket list. A few years, maybe a decade, down there would give him distance. Give him what he needed.

The fresh scent of a bakery filled the air, making Alexander a bit nauseous—or it could be the butterflies in his stomach forcing their way out.

"This is it," Stephan said as they approached the gate of Dionora's parents' home that had a Christmas wreath hung on it. Alexander took a look around at the colored lights and the tiny tree decorated by the door. The wooden gate extended in either direction, turning into a retaining wall that circled the house and a yard with just enough land that you couldn't reach out and touch the neighbor's house. The home was two stories and had at least three bedrooms, with a flower–lined walkway leading to the rustic green front door.

The house resembled a Snow White–looking home in the middle of a grotto. "Quite nice. The family seems to be doing very well. A chateau in Paris, how bad can this really be?"

Alexander's heart sank as he compared the home to what the family had had nearly a century ago in Venice. Decades had passed. One married son and one daughter still not tied in wedlock—but both probably still living at home. No rich in–laws, no extra land or possessions had been gained other than what lay here in front of them. The family was mired in mediocrity, and Alexander had done that to them.

He swallowed long and hard before reaching for the doorbell. "Let's get this over with."

CHAPTER 12

"So, no matter what, I'm not to approve of anything he does," Ricold said, sneaking a peek out the window and staring at the man who had broken his daughter's heart. With a harrumph, he added, "Shouldn't be too hard to do."

Dionora gently touched her father's arm, her fingers trailing down the sleeve of his button-down shirt, as she glanced out the window to see Alexander and Stephan. "You'll do fine, Daddy."

Dionora took in a deep breath and looked at her dress, straightening out any imaginary creases she thought she saw. The frock was lower-cut than most outfits she wore. It wasn't that she didn't have the bosom to pull off such a look, but more because of modesty. Today, and for the rest of the week, the *girls* would be on display.

"He's here?" Gisele asked as she placed a tray of coffee and accoutrements on the breakfast table. She carefully set out the placemats one-by-one, noting which setting was for Alexander.

Dionora fidgeted with her hair and inspected the simple table setting. "This is his seat?"

"And his drink," Edumund walked from the kitchen and placed a small container on the placemat. He nodded to Sarah, who carried in a similar container. "Stephan's is the same."

A smirk sprang to Dionora's face, causing her lips to twitch in an upright curl of defiance. "Then we're ready."

The door chime rang, and she ran upstairs so she could make her appearance.

Alexander heard heavy footsteps approaching the door. Knowing it would be Ricold, he held the flowers at chest level to give himself a barrier. The protection wasn't because Ricold was a strong vampire. He wasn't even as tall as Alexander, and Alexander had Stephan as backup. It was because this was a past father–figure to him, a man he had held respect for all his childhood—the one man he had hurt the most. He needed to be prepared for whatever greeting he had coming.

Ricold opened the door, his stiff body and hardened smile greeting Alexander. "So, let's get this done." He stepped aside to allow them entry, but Stephan held out his hand and stopped Alexander from taking a step inside the home.

"This is Alexander Marino. He has come to call on the lovely Dionora."

"No shit." Ricold frowned and shook his head in disapproval. "I've known you two bastards all your life. I was there when our *dear* friends gave birth to you." Ricold locked eyes with Stephan. "Your mother nearly died during your childbirth because of your big head. Good thing Gisele was a good midwife for vampires back in the day."

There was history. *Lots* of history between the three families. Alexander wasn't surprised by such a blow this early; he had just hoped the verbal tongue lashing would be kept to a minimum.

Stephan nudged Alexander's arm. "The card," he whispered.

Alexander handed Ricold his calling card: a simple name on fine, white cardstock printed the day before. "Does this help?"

Ricold took the card, and after a cursory glance, he crumpled it. "Doesn't hurt. Come in."

The two made their way into the home and past the decorated Christmas tree and other decorations. "That wasn't too bad," Stephan said as they were led to the breakfast table. "We're both still standing, and there was only one jab each to our families."

"So glad I brought the precious card," Alexander said, his voice laced with derision. "Wasn't I supposed to hand it to Dionora?"

"We're in the house. Take it as a win."

"There you are," Gisele said, moving the pot of coffee —one of the very few drinks vampires enjoyed—off the tray and onto the table. "I see you found your way to our small but satisfactory home."

"It's a lovely home," Alexander said, glancing around… doing anything to avoid making eye contact with the woman he used to call his second mother. "You've done quite nicely for yourselves."

"Haven't we, though?" Edmund beamed with delight as he crossed the room and offered his hand. "Only a few more payments, and we'll own the place."

Alexander's heart sank, but he shook Edmund's hand. "We thought we saw you the other night at the bar."

"My bar." Edmund's face hardened. "I own it. I saw you there. I didn't know you were in town to...to see my sister."

"Well..." Alexander cleared his throat. "There's no telling with the Verheirates Schlange which lovely lady will be on your list."

A pat on the back came from Stephan. Alexander turned to find the barmaid from the other night.

"You may remember my wife, Sarah. She waits tables at our bar."

Alexander and Stephan nodded hello, and Alexander wondered just how much she had heard. He had expected Dionora to reject him immediately. Was there something that he and Stephan had said that night, overheard by Edmund's wife, that would have caused Dionora to agree to marry him?

Soft footsteps behind him told Alexander that her father had fetched Dionora. At the very least, they could have their coffee, conclude their meeting, and have their rejection. Alexander would allow the family to throw him out of their house and humiliate him. It was the least he could do.

He just hoped that Ricold and Edmund wouldn't beat him up as they did so.

Alexander turned and immediately caught Dionora's gaze. Her stunning eyes, richly accented with a fine powder that made her cornflower–blue gaze as stunning as possible, caught the morning light from the window. She always had the most mesmerizing stare, one he could get lost in.

"Good morning," she said, smiling at him as if she had waited for this day to come her whole life. "Flowers? You shouldn't have."

"You told us to." Alexander hadn't even remembered that he carried them, but Gisele quickly took them from him and placed them into a vase on the table.

"Good morning, Dionora," Stephan said. "You look lovely."

No, she looked heavenly. The wintry air caused most humans to run for sweaters and thick frocks. But to a vampire, who wasn't concerned with such things, she wore a revealing summer dress—fresh and light, and... red, his favorite color. Her hair cascaded down in curls and fell upon her creamy shoulders where only the thinnest of spaghetti straps held up the dress across her beautiful curves.

"He brought a card," Ricold said, tossing the paper onto the table and taking a seat.

Her lips curled into a huge smile, one that caused a twinkle in her eyes and reminded him of how beautiful she looked when happy. "Here is mine." She plucked out a tiny white card hidden under her dress, tucked safely between the two fleshy mounds he had known so well. His manhood threatened to harden in response.

"Thank you." He took the card, which held just her printed name. "I do appreciate this."

For some reason, maybe due to the formality of it all, he placed the card into his pocket. It seemed like the proper thing to do, and right now, propriety felt right.

Alexander knew he should shut down his emotions. Just allow her to reject him, get her revenge, and then they could all get on with their lives. Instead, he took her hand and escorted her to the table where they all took their seats.

Ricold pulled out a sheet of paper and pen, his frown deepening. "Let's go down the list. Make sure you get everything right." He pointed at the crumpled paper on the table. "Card. Check." Glancing at the sheet once again, he said, "We are to have pleasantries around a beverage to get reacquainted."

"Ricold," Gisele said, her voice as fake–hostess–like as Alexander had ever heard it. "Don't be in such a rush. I'm dying to find out how Alexander is doing. I understand he got married and has a son now."

Stephan's eyebrow arched. "The marriage ended many years ago. The Council has cleaned up any ties with that family, and Alexander is free to enter into a new agreement with your daughter."

"Oh, I'm sure Alexander and his family took care of the first marriage. They're good at making sure they come out on top," Edmund said, his voice filled with hatred.

Gisele poured the cups of coffee and ignored his remark. "The carafes in front of you have blood to mix in with the pecan–flavored coffee." She smiled politely. "It's my usual morning cup. I hope you like it."

Alexander fixed his drink and took a sip, nearly gagging while the others hummed happy sounds from the backs of their throats. "This is delicious," he said, setting his cup down. He noticed Stephan grimacing, as well.

"So, tell us, how are you and your family doing?" Dionora asked.

~

After listening to Alexander tell the story of his father's near–death experience earlier that year, Dionora felt terrible for asking her mother to lace the vampire's drinks with turpentine. The poison wouldn't affect either Stephan or Alexander, but it would give them a nasty taste in their mouth. Now, she felt like she could have been the bigger person and offered them a real drink.

Thank goodness the mead remained corked. She opened the bottle and poured half the container into a carafe to warm it. She then placed the drink with a decanter of blood on a tray before carrying it to the back-yard. If they had been human, a plate of cookies or fine cakes would have joined the beverage.

She thought back to her pre–transitioning years when she and the boys could still eat human food. Alexander's mother certainly didn't cook, and they had servants for all their needs. Servants who would come and go from his life. They were mostly strangers to him. Alexander's mother had never felt the need to share their true nature with her human staff. She also never trusted an uncom-pelled human to not try and stake them in the middle of the night. Which meant that emotionally cold hands had raised Alexander.

Which is why he'd loved coming to Dionora's house all the time. Gisele was the best cook, best hands–on mom, and she doted on all the kids. Alexander loved the honey cakes her mom made that he ate until his stomach hurt.

If they still consumed human food, those honey cakes would likely be on the platter, as well.

But they didn't eat human food anymore. Dionora

smiled at the honey mead, which may be the closest they'd ever get to those past glory days. The honey would taste terrible now, but a connection existed there, and it made Dionora smile to remember the past she had once lived and lost.

She and Alexander walked the length of the deck, the wooden boards creaking under them. They then sat quietly on the wooden porch swing with the sunlight filtering down through the trees and giving them some shade. A moment of awkward silence existed where they listened to the birds chirping and the bench creaking as they slowly swung on the hard seat.

"I see you have a firepit," Alexander said, his nose sniffing the cold air.

Dionora also picked up the smoke residue from the pit. She pointed to the neat stack of firewood, which lay near some sparkling Christmas lighting, decorating the white trellis on the side of the porch. "We do our best to blend in as humans. During the colder months, we light a fire out here."

The two sat alone on the deck as her parents continued to torment Stephan—per Dionora's request. Right now, the vampire was probably out finding the next item on the must-do list of the morning's activities.

"I can understand your parents wanting you to be closer," Dionora said, referencing Alexander's father's accident. "A scare like that can cause you to rethink things."

She didn't want to think about losing her parents. Being immortal, you tended to forget that vampires could die, as well. And, even though Salvador wasn't her favorite person in the world, he didn't deserve that type of fate. "How fast was he driving?"

Alexander shook his head as he stared at the hanging flower baskets with their fake flowers, giving the porch some color. "Fast enough to nearly sever his head when the windshield..." His voice trailed off as his hand sliced toward his neck to indicate the gruesome detail.

"And you, the dutiful son, returned home to be with them."

"I'm a saint. What can I say?" His piercing, green eyes held hers briefly, and then his hand grazed her thigh in a move that she thought seemed too personal, though not aggressive. The touch was his way of connecting with her. It had always been his way.

She was still angry with him, and she didn't really want to, but she leaned in and gave him a half-hug. It seemed appropriate for the discussion. "You got scared?"

He glanced away. "He survived."

His voice, filled with love, touched her. He may be the man who'd hurt her, but he was still the same boy she'd grown up with. The same child who'd practically lived at her home, who had hopes and dreams of living a normal life.

One that didn't include her, but a life with meaning. Alexander had always wanted to make a difference in the world. From everything she had googled about him, and what little she could find on the internet or glean from old friends, he'd lived a superficial life filled with good times and nothing to show for it.

He wasn't better for their breakup. He was far worse.

A rustling sounded from the outside gate, followed by

Stephan escorting a young woman to the back porch. "This fulfills the next item on the list."

Stephan walked toward them with a human girl in tow.

Dionora chuckled. It had only taken the vampire a few hours to find the perfect person. Stephan had always been a good tracker as a kid, but this...this impressed Dionora. Hand–selected, with only two people in the town to truly meet—and only one that would exceed—the strict description her father had given for the Bridal Demand.

The specific requirement that Dionora had crafted for them to fail.

She looked into Henrietta's blank gaze. The small child followed Stephan obediently and without choice. She was a local peasant with not much money or prospects for the future, but she was a hardworking girl from a nice family, not unlike Dionora back in Venice so long ago.

The girl hadn't been hurt, and she certainly wouldn't remember what was going on, but Dionora took pity on her. If this had been a real betrothal gift of decades earlier, Dionora would have been hungry. She would have been pleased with the selection and would have eaten.

Thank goodness for bagged blood. Dionora had hated feeding from humans after her transition year. Her parents had taught her to hunt, and Stephan had shown her how to track like a predator. Alexander comforted her when she cried about having to sink her fangs into an unwilling—or at least unknowing—partner.

Listing the items on his fingers, Stephan said, "Your father said Alexander had to present to you a token of how he could provide for you as a future wife. I have found someone that is smaller in stature than you, someone who has an A+ blood type, someone who has never had measles, polio, or the other ten ailments your father demanded." He waved his hand at the compelled human, who wore one of the ugliest Christmas sweaters Dionora had ever seen. "This virgin does not drink, use tobacco, or any other illicit drug. Neither does she..."

Dionora allowed Stephan to continue the long list. She wasn't going to bite a sweet teenage girl who should be at school right now, but it did tell her just how far Stephan was willing to go as Alexander's best man.

"Do you know this child?" Alexander asked, apparently picking up on Dionora's smile.

"Mom delivered her." She smiled boastfully at the statement. "Mom delivered Henrietta's siblings, too." She waved her finger around. "In fact, she's helped deliver most of the babies born in this region over the last twenty–five years. She worked as a general practice doctor for a long time, and now she works as an obstetrician. She's thinking of doing genetic work in her next life."

A smile pulled up Alexander's lips, an expression filled with what Dionora suspected was genuine feelings. She wasn't sure if it was because of the familiar use of the name *Mom*, which she'd had no intention of saying, or maybe because Alexander was proud of her mother's accomplishments, as well.

"Shall I continue?" Stephan asked, irritation evident in the tone of his voice. "This girl has never had an operation, does not have a genetic mutation, has only eaten a regional diet..."

"*Mom* sounds like she's doing well," Alexander whispered in a low tone into her ear, and his warm breath brushed against Dionora's cheeks, causing her to flush with a familiarity she had thought long gone.

His hand waved at the child as Stephan's voice trailed on. "Is Henrietta the only one that would have satisfied this long list?"

"Shh." Dionora patted him gently on his leg. "She has a sister who only recently turned ten, so there were at least two," she said, quoting the age limit for all vampire bites allowed by the European Council.

"Two?" He snickered. "At least you gave Stephan a fighting chance." He now studied the girl who stood at full attention, blissfully unaware of what was going on. "Do you really intend to have her as a snack?"

Dionora pulled away slightly and saw his face pinched as though he remembered all the issues Dionora had had in the past while trying to feed.

"I mean," he said, pointing to his chest, "I still have two dry shoulders for you to cry on." His eyes blazed with a soulful hint of remembrance. A glance that held the secrets of how she had suffered all those years ago and had tried her best to fit in.

She patted his chest and smiled warmly. "I haven't fed that way in a long time." Her hand remained where it was, feeling his strength beneath her palm.

He placed his hand atop hers. "Now, why don't you fill me in on the rest of the family and how you're really doing?"

CHAPTER 13

"We don't want to be late." Alexander quickened his pace. They had met the parents so they could check that off the list. They had, for the most part, pleased the parents, as well. At least he hoped they had.

He walked across the street with determined strides to the flower shop and then paused as he stood in front of a single, perfect, red rose.

The petals matched the color Dionora's tight-fitting dress from yesterday, where the buttons were about ready to pop off because of the way the fabric held her breasts—stretched and barely contained.

She always had such beautiful breasts. Perfectly round. Pert nipples. Pristine and only touched by him—at least they had been back then.

A thorn from the rose pricked him, and the smell of his blood wafted in the air.

What was he doing?

His heart raced, and the beating echoed in his head,

rattling around and making him dizzy. He realized that he truly wanted to see Dionora again. Not just to talk pleasantries and drink whatever the hell Mom had decided to poison him with, but to honestly talk with *her*.

Alexander's hand raced to his stomach, thinking of the coffee he had drunk. Wretching after leaving their home had been unpleasant, but at least he hadn't thrown up in their flower garden on the way out. Today, he'd have to avoid drinking anything. Or, at the very least, keep a close eye on Mom.

He chuckled inwardly. *Mom*, now a caring doctor, had actually poisoned them. This was the woman who hadn't been able to kill the family of rats she had discovered living in her barn back in Venice. A woman who had gone out of her way to keep a cat about so she wouldn't have to do what she had deemed unsavory, but which was perfectly fine for...what was the name of her cat? Jezzy?

Dionora had always been crafty as a child, and now he knew where she'd gotten it from.

So, today's tasks were to avoid ingesting anything, get Dad to like him, and truly talk with Dionora again. The few moments they had shared on that porch swing, the way her hair had blown onto him, washing him in her sweet scent, and those eyes—piercing him with soulful knowing—had taken him back. Back to a time before their breakup when she had remained *his* Dionora. And only his.

"A single red rose?" Stephan asked, pointing to the bud nestled in Alexander's hand. "I think it's perfect."

The fangy, all-knowing smirk from his friend seemed a bit too much to deal with this morning. "She loves roses."

"Then, by all means, let's buy this single beauty—the perfect token of your affection—and get onto the second meeting and the dowry acquisition."

Alexander removed the rose from its bucket in front of the flower mart, his nose on overload with all the fragrant buckets of blooms. "There's to be a dowry?" He placed the money, more than enough for the purchase, onto the table where the merchant stood. "They don't have to pay a dowry for their daughter."

"Yep. They do. It's part of the agreement. Just like stomaching the poison yesterday, I'm sure there will be a catch for the dowry, too." Stephan took a deep breath and shook his head. "I threw up all over Henrietta's home when I tried to catch her. She was pretty fast."

Smiling, Alexander could only imagine that scenario. "Then you must be slowing down in your old age, my friend."

Stephan rubbed his belly. "It's all the bagged blood. I'm out of practice with hunting."

They continued their walk to Dionora's home, each step sloshing and soaking Alexander's boots since it had rained last night. "You mentioned a picnic today." Alexander glanced up at the sky. Rain never bothered him, but sitting near a stream, empty picnic basket in hand, and pretending to eat didn't sound like a good day to him.

"Today is more pleasantries, poetry reading, getting in good with the family…"

Alexander's hand tapped his coat pocket. The poetry book lay safely inside. God, he hoped he wouldn't have to spend the entire day reading. Reading poetry would only waste their time.

Dionora had opened up to him, and he liked it. Hopefully, today would be more of the same.

Her family was doing well, or at least she had indicated as much. Her career had taken her to America and to Canada, which were two places he'd spent little time in over the last few decades. Not because of her, but because he had always preferred Europe.

Now, he saw his travels as a price. He had no home. Oh, he had places to live and people and vampires to hang out with, but other than Stephan, Alexander didn't have many people in his life. Dionora loved her parents, and she seemed happy to live with them. Humans filled this town, individuals whom she not only lived and worked with but who she also spent time with. People who knew her and cared about her.

Dionora was the puzzle piece that fit. The one that fit squarely in the center with the picture that completed the entire image surrounding it. Her parents, her brother, her friends…all of them were the outer edges that gave her structure in the puzzle.

And Alexander was the lost toy, perhaps even a broken one, that only Stephan would play with.

"I forgot to mention one thing," Stephan said as they approached Dionora's home. "Today's outing is an all–day affair."

"All day?" Alexander didn't mind spending the day with Dionora. In fact, the idea quite pleased him. It had been the slightly giddy sound to Stephan's voice that worried him.

"You'll be fine." Stephan knocked on the door. "I'm no longer required to present you formally to the family since we took care of that yesterday." Stephan smiled up at his friend and patted him on the back. "Today, it's all up to you."

Alexander wasn't sure if that was a threat or a promise, but the door opened, and he didn't have time to ask.

"Please, come in," Ricold said, his voice not quite so laced with rigidity as he glanced at the clouds in the sky. "Gisele is in town delivering a baby, so it's just us today."

Dionora straightened the fabric of her dress and pressed her hand over her hair one more time to smooth it out. The mirror, unfortunately, cast a fuzzy reflection, but she could tell enough that her makeup looked fine.

Her original plan was to wear whorish makeup, or maybe none at all. The option depended on how shallow of a vampire Alexander turned out to be, and which would displease him more.

She applied red lipstick to her full lips, allowing them to plump with whatever Maybelline had come up with. Leaning in, she inspected the crimson smile she now wore, the modern cosmetic industry pleasing her.

Puckering, she blotted her lips and caught the excess in a tissue. She had bought the lipstick yesterday after Alexander had left, an even brighter shade that she knew he'd notice. She'd bought it so that he'd be enticed to kiss her lips.

She felt a growing need within her, and a flush cascaded over her skin.

A kiss.

She remembered his passionate kisses of the past.

How his lips had felt when they brushed up against hers and nibbled. And sucked. And traveled.

Roamed to her neck, her chest, and oh so many other places.

His tender, well–crafted, and beautiful lips.

She squeezed her inner thighs together and felt a throbbing for a man that, just last week, she would have staked. How was it that Alexander could get under her skin so easily? How was it that he had always been the only one to do so?

And now, the two were betrothed. Caught up once again in the drama of his family and life.

She let out a deep breath that she didn't know she'd been holding. She needed to stick with the plan. She had just started a new job with better pay and prestige. She was back home again with her parents and brother.

She didn't need any turmoil right now.

She didn't need her life uprooted for the second time this year.

She didn't need Alexander.

She walked down the stairs, hearing the sound of his voice as he talked with her father. At the very least, she had to save her dad from the pathetic small talk.

"Dad, I think we can forgo a picnic in the rain today," she said as she entered the living room and saw her father pushing an empty basket into Alexander's hands and telling him that the list needed to be fulfilled. The Bridal Demands could always be amended.

Alexander looked adorable, his hair wet with a curl of a bang across his forehead. It gave him a Superman appearance, and she'd always liked the man of steel.

"I set out the mead but didn't prepare it," her father

said, slightly turning and raising an eyebrow so only she could see.

"I'll take care of it." She walked to the kitchen and poured the drink into a decanter to warm it. Drinks in the kitchen at ten in the morning? Yeah, she could do that. It was five o'clock somewhere, right? Maybe.

CHAPTER 14

"So, Bianca wasn't exactly who you thought she was," Dionora said as the two of them sipped their mead alone on the porch swing.

It had been the undiscussed topic in the room, the white rhino so to speak, bullish and dominant. Alexander knew they'd eventually get around to talking about his ex-wife, the one he had tossed Dionora aside for. He only wished there had *never* been a time when another woman came between them.

Alexander briefly gazed into Dionora's eyes and found the unanswered questions he didn't want to see but needed to answer. "I never loved her the way I loved you."

Her lips pursed, and he noticed a glint of moisture in her eyes as she glanced away. Was his confession what she had wanted to hear? Or, did it hurt her even more?

"She wasn't who anyone thought she was," he said, his voice soft and distant with a hint of dismissiveness. Bianca was the reason he hadn't married Dionora, the reason he hadn't spent the last few decades sharing his life with her, and the reason his son had blond hair and Mediterranean brown skin instead of peaches–and–cream skin like Dionora's.

"And you have a son." Dionora's voice sounded soft, as if the thought of Alexander having sex with another woman and producing an heir still stung her deeply, but she had a smile on her face as though she were happy for him. "I'm sure you're a wonderful father."

A father spends time with his kid. He nurtures and loves them. Even though Alexander had tried to be there for his son, Bianca's family and their wishes had always come first. The boy went to boarding school, then trade school, and now ran their family business.

His son became a member of *their* world, not his. Often, Alexander felt more like a sperm donor than a father. His choices for his son were ignored, his wishes for the child cast aside, and his role diminished until he finally left the marriage and his son behind.

"A child placed in *her* family tree completed the marriage contract. We never got around to placing a second child in my lineage."

All vampire lines were single branches in a never-ending family tree. Like royalty, only one child won the inheritance game. Siblings, which the Council kept to a minimum, got unfair treatment and usually no blood supplies from their government. The Council maintained the population and wealth distribution this way.

Alexander figured the budding branch under him would remain empty.

Dionora took a deep breath and let it out, her words whispering across his face with sincerity. "I'm sorry."

He held her hand, interlocking their fingers and

feeling the coolness of her vampire touch. "I'm glad we only produced one child. Bianca got my family's money, land, and prestige. She got the heir she wanted. And she never gave up her lovers or her high demands. The marriage ended after the ten–year provision she needed for the land acquisition. She strung me along for years, and, in truth,"—he paused, feeling the prickling sting of truth about to come out—"I'm not sure Enrico is my son."

The pain of the declaration shot through him and settled in his chest where it lay heavily. He had never admitted that to anyone before, not even to Stephan. Although, Stephan, as well as others, suspected as much. Alexander had never tested the boy, never planned to either. He liked the idea of having a child, and he couldn't blame Enrico.

"My God." Her free hand raised to her mouth, and she let out a gasp. "That's awful."

He didn't want Dionora's pity. He didn't deserve it. "And you? You never had a child?" he said, quickly changing the topic.

A flush came to her face before she looked away and gently shook her head. "Nope." She let out a slightly nervous sigh. "I wanted that happy marriage first and just never got it."

She would have been a wonderful wife and mother. He knew that having made love to her and then tossing her aside had ruined her reputation in the Council's eyes. Any others going through the Verheirates Schlange looking for a mate would see that she was not a virgin. In a soft-ened voice, he said, "One broken engagement..."

"Three."

He stared at her. "Three?"

"You were the first, and that was through the Council. The second was a vampire of my choice, but that didn't work out. He only used me to make a woman he loved jealous."

She sipped her mead, pausing, he figured, to allow the news to settle in.

"Number three came from the Verheirates Schlange again, but at the last minute, he literally stood me up at the altar."

There had been three. Three broken proposals, and no marriage. No children. No happily ever after for Dionora.

Alexander's mind raced as he tried to understand that she and her wonderfulness had been passed up so many times. A treasure like her, who *should* have been snapped up immediately, had waited her entire life for what he had callously thrown aside.

"I had no idea."

"That's why my name remained in the database and available for selection for your list. I've been there nearly ten years, waiting. The last rejection placed me at the bottom of the selections—you know, since I'm high–risk —and my name hasn't seen the light of day until you showed up."

She took a big gulp of her mead, finishing her glass. "Oh, look," she said, holding it up. "Time for a refill."

He watched as she got herself another drink and tried to shrug off what he could only imagine she thought of as her disgrace. In his heart, Alexander knew that while her family may be poor, they believed in what was proper. For her to marry, and have children, she needed to find someone on the Verheirates Schlange. And, currently, that list deemed her unworthy.

He took the glass from her hand and set it on the table, catching her off guard. Leaning back with her onto the hard swing porch, he placed his arm around her shoulders and held her tight.

"You're too good for that damn list," he said, wanting to make her feel better. Wanting to make everything all right.

He heard a quiet sniffle from her. Glancing down into her soft blue eyes, he saw the woman he had fallen in love with. The woman he *still* loved.

His heart raced, and he found it difficult to breathe. After all these years, she was in his arms once again. He looked at her full, red lips, only mere inches from his own. His hand cradled her face, and her gaze traveled to his lips.

He leaned in and softly touched her velvety, kissable mouth with his.

Her hand touched his shoulder, and he shifted his body to hold her more securely against his. Her response was to add pressure to their kiss and deepen it.

It was pure heaven.

The door to the house creaked open, and the two of them broke apart. Dionora sat straighter on the swing and ran her hand through her hair.

"You need to catch a train in an hour," Ricold said, peeking out at them. He studied them for a moment and then gave Dionora a questioning expression.

"Hi, Daddy," she said. "Is there something you needed?"

If her father had seen the kiss, he kept it to himself. Alexander was sure that Ricold would question her later about it and add a warning against getting too emotionally involved with a man she, or likely the entire family, intended to publicly shame with a formal rejection.

"Can I bring in the surprise?" Ricold asked.

"Yes, Daddy. Of course."

And so, the next step in the insults continued. The kiss had been real, though. At least it was for Alexander. In his heart, he wanted to believe that it was genuine for her as well and not just another game.

She pulled away, wiping her lips with the back of her hand—smearing the rest of her lipstick. "That was a mistake." She gazed up at him briefly, but then looked away. "We shouldn't have kissed."

The words stung, but before he could ask for an explanation, Ricold carried over a box and set it on the floor near the patio table. He caught the fact that the two still sat closely together, and his stern expression told Alexander how much he didn't appreciate the familiarity between him and Ricold's daughter.

Ricold cleared his throat. "As you know, it is customary to provide a dowry."

Sitting straighter, but still keeping his arm around Dionora, Alexander said, "A dowry is unnecessary, sir."

He added the *sir* for good measure. The virtual daggers still coming from the man's gaze unsettled Alexander, and he wondered how much ass–kissing would be needed for Ricold to crack a halfway decent smile.

"Yes, it is." Ricold's face pinched as he glared at Alexander. "We like to honor *our* requirements in this household."

Evidently, it would require a lot of ass–kissing for this man to lose some of his anger. Duly noted.

"The family Tudor, presents to your family, Marino,"

Ricold said, reaching into the box and grabbing the tiny animal, "one token of livestock."

Ricold pulled the creature out of the box and handed it to Alexander, who sat up and accepted it.

"You're giving us a hamster?"

"It's a toy pig, although a runt and quite small yet." Dionora smiled at the pink babe and added, "We call him Walter."

"Not Wilber?" Alexander asked, knowing that Dionora had always enjoyed stories as a child and suspected that *Charlotte's Web* was one of her later favorites.

She looked into the pig's eyes. "He is more of a Walter."

The pig squealed in his arms, so Alexander handed it to Dionora. "So...pet, not hors d'oeuvre for human guests."

Dionora slapped him on the leg, which gained the attention of her father once again.

With a frown that creased his face, Ricold said, "It's a pet, moron. And it's customary to accept a gift graciously."

Quickly plastering on a fake smile, Alexander nodded. "Quite right, sir. My family is thrilled to accept Wilber... I mean, Walter."

"Right." Ricold stared at his daughter as if there were something else to say or do. The list still had items on it, and Stephan had been vague this morning with that itinerary. Alexander couldn't wait to see what was next on the agenda.

"That's fine, Daddy. Thanks for bringing him out." She settled the tiny pig in her lap and it laid down with her gentle touch.

Once Ricold left, Alexander wasn't sure what to do since they'd have to leave soon for the train. Should he talk about the kiss? Should he try to recapture the moment? He finally decided to place his arm around Dionora once again and used his free hand to pat the tiny pig. "This suits."

"It does?" Her mischievous gaze sought out his eyes, letting him know that the games continued. "How so?"

"A dowry is from the daughter's parents to convince a man to take the burden of their child as a wife." Alexander shook his head. "Any man would be happy to have you. A dowry is unnecessary."

"It's customary, that's all."

"On the other hand, Arabian stallions, wild zebras, and a pride of lions should be given to your family for having them part with such a treasure as you."

CHAPTER 15

There had been no talk of that wonderful kiss other than for Dionora telling him that it was a mistake. She didn't mention how wonderful it had felt to be close to him again, how amazing it felt to be in his arms, or how delightful it felt to kiss him once more.

She'd made sure they didn't go down that route.

After putting Walter back in his crate and saying goodbye to her family—with no time for a lecture from her father—she and Alexander gathered her suitcases and made it to the train station just in the nick of time.

The two of them always seemed to be out of time, or out of sync.

Dionora touched her lips, still swollen from the passion she had felt. Alexander always knew how to kiss her so that she wanted more. And, right now, sharing this small train compartment—and the single bed with him— was all she could think about.

They had never had any issues when it came to things in the bedroom. Heat traveled down her body and settled in her core just thinking about how Alexander had pleasured her in the past. Her breath hitched, and she squeezed her thighs together. The good times with him had always been incredible.

Dionora stared at the hideaway bed hanging on the wall.

Alexander would be here soon.

The rotten bastard.

She still had unanswered questions. She understood why he felt obligated to honor his parents' wishes, but he had practically left her at the altar in order to marry another woman. He'd even had a child with Bianca.

Dionora closed her eyes, and a tear escaped. After all these years, without a single word from him, he thought that all would be forgiven?

Under no circumstances was she going to allow him to touch her. The kiss and the stolen embraces had been moments of weakness, that's all. She needed to stick to the plan. Continue her revenge. Get back at the man who had betrayed her.

She had packed five suitcases, some with heavy bricks, just to make the trip more frustrating. Now, looking at how much space they took up in her tiny train compartment, she regretted that foolish joke. She could barely move.

But tight–fitting, close quarters was what she had asked for. With the nightgown she had brought, and only one bed in the room, Alexander would know exactly what he had missed out on. What he would always miss out on.

She just needed to figure out which suitcase had her actual clothes in it.

A knock sounded on the door, and she quickly looked

at her watch. Alexander was an hour early. She side–stepped her luggage and made her way to the door, opening it carefully.

"Stephan?"

He stepped in without waiting for an invitation. Probably because he knew she wouldn't offer one.

"Is the compartment exactly as you wanted?"

Small, cramped, and intimate? It was perfect for her revenge.

"It's fine." She and Alexander were supposed to meet Stephan at the train station, but because they were late, Stephan had already registered and found his cabin. "Did you get settled in?"

"Yep. No problem." He looked at the suitcases, and she could tell that he was counting in his head. They were only going to be in Italy for a short time. One overnight bag would have been sufficient.

"You can tell Alexander that he's welcome to join me in an hour." That would give her enough time to slip into something more comfortable and completely off–limits.

The train jostled, and Dionora lost her footing in the tiny room, her hand catching the bedrail of the pull–down berth before she nearly fell.

"Looks like it might be a bumpy ride," Stephan said, holding out his hand to steady her. A slight chuckle escaped his lips, and his head nodded toward where Alexander would be. "I'm sure Alexander just spilled a drink all over himself."

"This train has a bar?" Alexander finding one did not surprise her. He'd had a drink in his hand pretty much since coming back into her life. That wasn't how she remembered him.

"Dining car. He likes to drink while traveling." Stephan nodded, and his eyebrow flexed upward. "He likes to drink *a lot* while traveling."

She let out a sigh, feeling guilt bubble up within her for the games she was playing. She never would have guessed that Alexander drank as much as he did, and she wondered how big of a role she played in that. "Does he often turn to alcohol?"

With a dismissive shrug, one that she didn't believe, Stephan said, "We travel a lot."

"But this trip. Seeing me…" She pointed at herself as if it weren't clear what she had meant. She felt her face pinch with worry. "Is he drinking more because of me?"

"The mead was extra. I think he finished the first bottle the second day." Stephan paused, and for a moment, Dionora saw concern in his expression that she hadn't seen before. "He's drinking a lot this trip, but it shouldn't be your concern."

Stephan waved his hand dismissively in the direction of the dining car. "He'll be fine, even if he drinks them out of their entire stock of alcohol by morning, his vampire constitution can handle it."

She understood that a vampire could drink a bartender out of all the booze they had on hand and still manage to walk a straight line. She didn't like that Alexander turned to drinking at all. At least, she didn't like the idea that he was drinking because of her.

Gazing around the room, she said, "It's nice to travel by train. Thanks for setting it up." She lowered the bed and placed her heavy bags atop it, hoping to change the subject. "I can't believe you couldn't get a direct route to Venice."

"Weird, huh?"

"I'm pretty sure there are direct routes."

Stephan shrugged. "I guess it was just meant to be that we take the scenic route." He gazed out the dark window as if anticipating the sights they'd see tomorrow. "I'm sorry if leaving a day early messed up any plans you had." He gave her a knowing nod. "You know, all the running about you've had us do."

"I'm sure I don't know what you're talking about," she said, not making eye contact, and with a slight lilt to her voice that said she knew exactly what he meant. "When do we arrive in Venice?"

"We'll be in Italy the day after tomorrow. We'll rent a car and arrive at the family villa in plenty of time for the party on the night of the new moon."

That gave Dionora just enough time to steel her nerves before seeing Alexander's parents again.

"I am sorry," Stephan said, helping her with her luggage. He looked at the bags questioningly for a second, probably wondering why they were so heavy. "I'm sorry for how things between us ended. You were a good friend, and once Alexander's family decided on Bianca, you—and your entire family—disappeared from my life. I never meant for you to lose me as well in the entire fiasco."

Her body stiffened as she listened to his soft and thoughtful words. She could feel tears coming to her eyes, but she held them back. "You were always more Alexander's friend than mine," she said in a chipper, it's–all–water–under–the–bridge tone.

He touched her arm and got her full attention. Now staring into her eyes, he said, "But we were friends. Good friends."

They had been. The three of them being a somewhat pre–pubescent vampire three Musketeers at the time. Their plans to go to college, travel the world together, and never let anything come between them were quickly severed when Bianca came into their lives.

"I've missed you," Stephan said. "I hope we can continue to be friends now." His jaw flexed, showing the tension in his face. "No matter what happens between you and Alexander, I don't want to lose you again. Running all over France and playing your games this past week, I've had more fun than you can ever imagine."

His eyes held sincerity, something he had always had as a child. Dionora leaned into him and hugged him tightly. "Friends till the end." She whispered their childhood saying into his ear as she held him close.

She took a deep breath and pulled away, giving him a huge smile in the process. But the severe look in his eyes, and the harsh expression he now wore told her that something was wrong.

"As a friend, I want to ask you something." His voice wavered, and his expression turned his boyhood good looks into that of a concerned adult. Someone worried about a very real problem that she knew would involve Alexander.

She wasn't sure what exactly she wanted, and now Stephan stood inches from her, not moving, with a dreaded, unasked question hanging in the air.

"I see how you look at him. The stolen glances that you think no one notices." Stephan visibly swallowed a lump in his throat and narrowed his eyes at her. "Do you still have feelings for him?"

Glancing away, she found it difficult to look at him. It

was the one question she dreaded him asking, and the one she'd known he would. She took a deep breath to stall.

He touched her gently on the chin and turned her head so she faced him. "He still has feelings for you."

She let out her breath quickly and felt the room spinning. Her knees grew weak, and she found herself having trouble balancing with the swaying of the train. She had wanted to torture Alexander for a bit, reject him and his parents openly and publicly, not stir up long–buried feelings. Feelings that, despite what she'd expected, some part of her—deep down—hoped were genuine.

"He had his chance with me years ago before he cast me aside." Her voice sounded a bit snider than she had intended, but she raised her chin and held her ground.

"His parents rejected you, he just went along with them." Stephan sat on the bed and patted the cushion, inviting her to join him. "You don't know how hard letting you go was for him."

Her heart pounded, and she felt flushed. Tears threatened to escape, but she held them back as she joined Stephan on the bed. In the most bitter tone she could muster, she said, "He made his bed and laid down with Bianca before my family left Venice in shame."

"He was preoccupied with the wedding and then moving to Budapest for ten years to fulfill the marriage contract…but he was hurting. I don't think he ever forgot you and the love you shared."

"It was so unfair." Dionora sniffled and looked away, hiding a reflection of the worst pain she had ever known that she knew would show in her eyes.

"It was unfair," Stephan agreed. "You were the local

vampire girl. The girl next door." He caught a quick glimpse of her as she looked into his eyes. "At the time, everyone went through the Council and the Verheirates Schlange because girlfriends and boyfriends were always included in the ten vamps selected."

She thought about the current process, the one she'd been taught with her new job. "It's all done with computers now. Back then, the local matchmaker would ask who the bride or groom fancied, who else in the town and neighboring towns was available, and they'd make the list."

"That's right," Stephan said. "You were manually added to Alexander's list. You were picked... It was a no-brainer. Even Alexander's parents thought your marriage would go through. That is until their sire forced them to honor the initial agreement she had made with them when she turned them."

That day still haunted Dionora. Alexander had come to her house to tell her that he had to marry someone else. He'd had no idea there was an arrangement between the two houses. Even his parents had thought the debt null and void because they had waited so long to have a child.

But Bianca's mother had turned both Isabella and Salvador, and, evidently, she was someone high up in the Council who could make their lives miserable. She discovered that the Marinos had a son and that he intended to marry another. Alexander's parents needed to honor the agreement they'd made with her. Their son would marry her daughter, or the family would suffer.

Thinking back to how barbaric vampires used to be with their hunting and territorial rights, Dionora could only imagine what the punishment would have been had they refused.

Stephan held her hand. "I stayed with him in Budapest to help him move on. He never loved Bianca, and he could never really let you go."

Let her go? He definitely *had* let her go—in the worst way possible. A man can say so much, love so strongly, and yet still have a child with someone he doesn't love? Alexander was a man in every sense of the word. Good-looking, rich, with a charming charisma. "He had a son with Bianca within the ten–year agreement," she said, countering Stephan.

Tears came to her eyes. "He had a baby with *her*."

"That baby was a contractual obligation." Stephan's eyes widened as he noticed a tear on her cheek. "Alexander had ten years to fulfill that specific agenda item, and that child barely came in time."

Contractual? Getting into bed with someone and creating a new life should never be put into such base terms. She felt as though she were wearing a corset, and she hadn't worn one of those torture devices in decades. She fought to take a deep breath and then let it out slowly as she wiped away a tear. "You don't understand." A sob escaped. "You don't get it."

"Wait." He leaned in so he could study her, his penetrating stare taking her in. "You're more upset about the baby than the union of the two."

Her heart tore.

"Of course, I'm upset." Stephan was a man, he wouldn't understand. Hell, sometimes, *she* didn't comprehend her irrationality when it came to Alexander.

"I promise, the baby has nothing to do with you."

It had *everything* to do with her.

"It was supposed to be *my* baby." She gasped, wanting the truth to return and hide within her dark pain again, deeply locked away. "*I* was supposed to have that baby with him. We were supposed to be a family." She looked into Stephan's eyes, the eyes of the boy who had once known her secrets and had kept them. "Alexander had a baby with someone else."

Stephan's eyes softened, and a pained expression covered his face. In a hushed, only–for–her–ears type of way, he uttered, "He didn't."

The air left the room, and she couldn't breathe. "What?" There had been a child. Enrico had been born within the arranged time limit. Not only had mutual friends told her about the birth, but she had seen the birth certificate at work when pulling Alexander's records, and he had mentioned the boy himself.

"Alexander didn't have a child with Bianca," Stephan repeated. The silence grew between the two of them. Stephan took a deep breath and then let it out slowly, repeating his words carefully. "*He* didn't have a child with Bianca."

The room seemed to have grown smaller, and her heart had started to rattle inside her chest, making her dizzy. "No." She stared into Stephan'seyes, knowing the truth.

"Oh, God. No." She stood up and gave herself distance from Stephan. She pointed a finger at him. "Do not say what I think you're saying."

"Alexander wasn't fulfilling the contract. At least, not within the time limit he was required to."

Her body stiffened, and she shook her finger

nervously at him. "So you…?" She studied him, looking him up and down, disgusted by what he had done. "Does Alexander know?"

"That I'm Enrico's father? No."

It felt silly, but knowing that Stephan had slept with Bianca as well added to Dionora's pain. Both of them. Not only had Alexander tossed Dionora aside for the bitch, but Stephan had also slept with her—not that there had ever been anything between the two of them.

"You never thought it wrong to sleep with your best friend's wife?" Dionora had never thought to feel sorry for Bianca, or ever call her *wife* instead of bitch, but what the hell had Stephan been thinking?

"What? No. It wasn't like that. Alexander knew about the affair."

The affair. God, it got worse by the minute. It was a full–blown affair? Couldn't it have been a test–tube baby? "Alexander knew and was fine with you fucking his wife?"

"Yes." Stephan stared at her. "Of course, he knew. I wouldn't hurt him like that. He's my best friend; he's like a brother to me."

Her hands went to her ears as though it were too much to listen to. But she wanted—no, she *needed*—to hear it all. She took a deep breath. "So you…?"

"Bianca had a long line of lovers. I was just one of many."

"But you're Enrico's father?"

"According to the DNA tests." He nodded his head as though it had been nothing. "We needed to leave Budapest and get on with our lives. That wasn't going to happen unless she had a baby. Besides," he added as matter–of–

factly as possible, "you work at the Verheirates Schlange, you know what happens when a marriage contract isn't fulfilled."

She had only just started working there, but it had been part of her training, and she knew the consequences. "An arranged marriage has ten years for any contractual obligations to be fulfilled, a love marriage not done through the Council has a twenty–five–year span."

Stephan's eyebrow rose. "But, if the contract *isn't* fulfilled?"

She let out an exasperated sigh. "They separate with the person who didn't meet the contract getting screwed in the divorce."

He held up his finger. "Now, yes. But Alexander was married when divorce was quite taboo."

Dionora had read something about the older contracts, but couldn't remember much about them—other than the fact that the penalties were severe. "What was in his contract?"

"Alexander would lose all legal rights. If Bianca wanted to reset the timer for another ten years, or even make the time fifty years, it was up to her discretion. Even if—"

Now remembering the older contracts and their wording, Dionora finished his sentence. "Even if they decided that the marriage would be forever."

Stephan's eyes widened. "Exactly. Bianca wasn't going to let Alexander go. He was the only man who didn't want her, and that made him so much more appealing to her. She made it quite clear that he was her favorite pet, and she loved to torture him because of his lack of interest. He would remain in that marriage until his dying day."

Shit. It was so archaic, but the word *divorce* had only been whispered and used as rumor back then. No one, especially a woman, wanted to go through it. And there had been several older marriages that had fallen into this horrific category.

Wait. Her mind raced back and thought of the words Stephan had just said. "What do you mean, he didn't want her? Are you saying they never consummated their relationship?" She thought back to what Alexander had said about not being sure the boy was his. Clearly, they had slept together.

"No." He paused. "I mean, yes, they...of course, he tried to fulfill the contract." He rubbed his forehead and took a deep breath. He then stared off blankly as if thinking of what to say next. "What I'm about to tell you stays between us."

Insider secrets about Alexander? "Of course." She sat back down on the bed with him.

"You're not going to want to hear this, but Alexander remained faithful to Bianca during their marriage."

Her jaw tightened. Stephan was right, she *didn't* want to know that. She then narrowed her eyes and shook her head, not believing what she had just heard. "You're telling me that, even though she slept around, he didn't?"

Stephan shook his head. "Never."

She stared at the wall across from the bed, her body tight. "I'm guessing the bitch was fantastic in bed."

A guilty and all-knowing smile crossed his lips. "She was talented, but that's not what I meant." He took a deep breath, let it out slowly, and paused as though selecting his words carefully. "I'm telling you that, even though their relationship wasn't a very passionate one, he remained true to her."

"Not very passionate?"

"Let's say he was contractually passionate, just enough to get the job done." He shrugged. "Until *I* got the job done for him."

A bubble of happiness struck her, and suddenly she felt like a weight had been lifted from her chest. All those years that she had imagined him and Bianca together having quiet moments, sharing secrets that only they understood, and making love. None of those were true.

But, Alexander had always been a very physical lover, at least with her. The two of them couldn't keep their hands off each other. "So he honored his marriage even though he hated the woman. It serves him right for dumping me for her."

"Exactly what he thought."

Stephan always had soulful eyes, and in them, she saw the pain he felt for Alexander.

"He remained true to a woman he hated and suffered for years because he felt as if he needed to pay penance for what he did to you."

Dionora liked the idea of Alexander feeling the need to pay penance. She had cried a river of tears over his marriage, so why shouldn't he suffer, as well? "Is that you assuming, or did he tell you that?"

"Alexander shares a lot when he's drunk."

And he did drink a lot. At least he did now. "I don't even remember him drinking when we were together."

"He developed the habit during his marriage. And even afterward when he finally became free to date anyone he wanted."

So the rumors were true. She had googled and asked questions while researching him for the Verheirates Schlange. He always seemed to have some hot vampire chick on his arm, at least for a while until someone else struck his fancy. His escapades were a who's–who sort of list, with wealthy vampire women all waiting for their chance with him.

"So you knocked up Bianca to get the contract fulfilled so he could end the marriage and the two of you could go off whoring the world?"

"Whoring the world?" He stared at her, a hurt expression on his face. "Where did that come from?"

She waved her hand in front of his chest. "You two going trollop hunting after you knocked up your best friend's wife. You don't think that's whoring around?"

"When you say it like that, it sounds terrible. I'd like to think that what I did was kind of noble."

"Noble? Holy fuck. I see why Alexander drinks."

The two stared at each other for several minutes, and then Stephan said, "If it makes you feel better, he's never questioned Enrico's paternity."

"He told me that he doesn't think he's the father, so he *does* question it."

Stephen's eyebrow disappeared beneath his hairline. "But not on paper."

"Of course, not. He'd bring shame to…" And then she understood. Shame on both houses, Alexander's and Stephan's. First the dishonor of not fulfilling the contract, and then the embarrassment of the affair. Bianca would be the innocent victim and probably get all of Stephan's family's riches in the process. Plus, she could still claim that the contract wasn't fulfilled and trap Alexander.

"She played you."

Stephan shrugged. "I doubt that was her original intent. I think she did want Alexander's baby, but settled for mine. Enrico is on her family line, and with no question over paternity, everything is completely legal."

"And Bianca would rather claim her son as a Marino than as part of your family." It now made sense why Bianca had allowed the marriage to dissolve after the ten-year clause. She didn't want either man, just the riches of Alexander's family and a child. If she claimed that the child wasn't Alexander's, she could trap him, but not get his family's money. Letting Alexander out of the marriage was the price she paid for her secret.

Dionora studied Stephan. "But you have a son. Does Enrico know?"

"No, which is good since the rich brat hates me." A guttural growl escaped from the back of his throat. "He's a spoiled heir to Bianca's fortunes. I'd rather have nothing to do with him."

"So Bianca got her heir, she got Alexander's riches and titles, and...did she ever love you?"

Stephan's face paled as if he'd never considered the question before. Or, perhaps, he didn't think he deserved love. Dionora wasn't sure how to read his face, but she felt pity for her old friend nonetheless.

"No. She never loved me, but that's how much I love Alexander."

Bianca really was a bitch. She had come between Dionora and the two men in her life, had kept them apart for decades. Dionora studied her friend and remembered the gangly little kid she once had known who had felt awkward and shy talking with girls. "You're a dad." A smile crept to her face, followed by a chuckle. "I can't imagine you having sex, let alone being a father."

His face lit up, and for a moment, he looked like the teenager she once knew. "Gee, thanks for that." In a more serious tone, he added, "I have a daughter in England and another son in Germany." His lips curled into a proud smile. "Alexander and I travel a lot now, and I do have good relationships with them." His voice trailed off, but then he added, "Regardless of Enrico, I love my children. I'm not a heartless father."

Her arms flung out, and she found herself hugging him before she knew it. "That thought never crossed my mind. I'm sure you're a great dad."

"I needed you to know about Enrico." Stephan took a deep breath. "Just in case it matters to you and plays into you marrying Alexander."

In her heart, she knew the truth made a difference. She felt sorry for Stephan, but a part of her was thrilled that Alexander had not had a child with that bitch. Of course, on paper he had.

"And, in case it makes a difference," Stephan said, smiling at her, "there is only one woman in this world that matters to Alexander. Only one female who is off–limits romantically to everyone but him."

For a moment, she was afraid to even think that the woman was her. She held her breath, afraid he may say someone else.

"Dionora, you're the only woman Alexander has ever cared about. He even forbade me from reading the file on you that you gave him."

A flood of tears was about to come, but they were mixed with years worth of harsh thoughts about how much she'd told herself that she hated Alexander. Her heart bubbled with emotions she'd thought were long gone, but there was still one unanswered question left.

"I can understand why he left me. I can even..."—she searched for the right words—"feel sorry for him for being in such a marriage. But he still needs to explain something to me."

Stephan's eyes lit up. "Maybe I can—"

"No," she said sternly, cutting him off. "I need to hear the answer from him, even if I have to torture him all night to get it."

Stephan let out a deep sigh, one that told her that enough was enough. "You've done a good job tormenting him. I don't think he's been this flustered in years. But go easy on him. He loves you so much. I'm sure he'll tell you anything you want to know."

She glanced at the ceiling and took a deep breath. "Not that his answer will make any difference. You know his parents will reject me the minute they see me," she said, her tone filled with worry. She didn't want to be hurt again.

"You don't know that they'll reject you."

She shook her head. "My family is financially worse off than when we were betrothed before. Trust me, they'll say no before I can even say hello to them."

His eyes narrowed. "And what if they say yes?"

"Not going to happen." Not in a million years would a hardworking purebred like her satisfy their lofty ideals for their son's wife.

"Alexander still loves you."

A longing tugged at her heart. Love or not, she still

didn't want to get hurt. "That didn't matter back then. I'm sure it won't matter now."

Stephan leaned in and got close. "This marriage contract is as legally binding as his last one was." A severity crept over him, one that she had never seen on him before. "I am delivering you to your future in–laws. It's up to you how serious you want to make this."

CHAPTER 16

*S*tephan led Alexander down the long corridor of the train. The canned, overhead lights reflected off the pale walls until they got to the connector pathway leading from one car to the other. Without the reflected light, the connector pathway's windows had a mirror effect. Alexander's reflection traveled with them in the dark windows that he passed. He paused a moment and studied his reflection since there was no silver in the window pane.

Handsome. Well–groomed. And a total schmuck.

"And you're positive she wants to spend the night with me?" Wanted. There had been many women who had wanted his attention over the years, but he had never figuratively stabbed them in the back.

How could she want him to spend the night with her? How could she even stand to look at him?

"Absolutely. And, according to the agenda, it is to be a chaste night."

Of course, they weren't going to make love. He was

going to be in a room with her all night and not touch her. Outside of them staying up all night playing board games, he wasn't sure how that would be possible—unless there were two beds and she chained him alone on one of them.

"And you are to remain fully clothed." Stephan pointed to the pajamas and the smoking jacket he wore. "Which is why we had to go shopping."

"I need a minute," Alexander said, pausing and still looking at his reflection.

He studied the smoking jacket and pajamas he wore, the ones outlined specifically in Dionora's list of required attire for the night. The pajamas were easily bought, but Stephan had to run all over town in search of the old-style smoking jacket. Just like all the other hoops he'd had to jump through.

Tonight was just another game to Dionora.

She had no idea how difficult it was for Alexander to be near her. For him to hear her laugh, see her smile, and not be able to touch her. He wanted so much to run his fingers through her hair, to smell the delicious scent of her skin, to kiss her soft lips again.

His thoughts went back to their hot, magical kiss. What was it about Dionora's lips that, with just one touch, had his entire body awakening with passion? Alexander had been with many women, both human and vampire since his marriage ended, but no one had ever touched his soul the way Dionora did.

He touched his own lips. He couldn't explain the kiss they'd shared, but her reaction after her father came to the porch did not surprise him. No one in that family wanted him back in their lives. Not after everything he had put them through in the past. She was, and would forever be, untouchable to him.

He paused and thought about that. She was the one woman that he wanted to touch, and the only one he couldn't.

But that only seemed fair after the way he had treated her.

He scowled at his reflection and then turned away so he couldn't see it anymore. He didn't want to hurt Dionora, but he had set her up to be devastated once again.

"Why didn't her family outright reject me? No one would have blamed them if they had. And yet, here we are, still following some silly agenda and taking Dionora to meet my parents."

"Maybe she plans to reject you in front of your family."

A heavy weight of guilt lifted from him. That was it. Dionora wanted the public display, wanted the parental shaming, and wanted to twist the knife as deeply as she could.

Good for her. Publicly humiliate the family that did the same to her. Then she could leave Venice a single woman and be on her merry way, never to see him again.

But he now knew where she lived. Knew where she worked. Knew how to reach her.

He desired to see her. Longed to touch her. To have her as his own. But he would have to honor her wishes. He and Stephan would have to move away and not cross the French border again. Maybe they could live in America. Although, he suspected an ocean wouldn't keep him from thinking of her.

"Do me a favor?" Stephan asked, his voice sounding

determined. "Answer all of her questions."

Was tonight a big Q&A session? "What do you mean?"

"Just answer all of her questions."

God damn it. Stephan knew something. Alexander always hated when secrets were kept from him. "What is she going to ask?"

Stephan shook his head. "I really don't know. She did say she had at least one unanswered question and that she needed to hear the answer from you."

They continued their trek to her compartment, with Alexander clueless to what the questions could be. Was it about his marriage? Would she even want to know anything about his time in Budapest? Was it about his son? He had already shared with her that he doubted the boy's parentage.

Carolers sang Christmas songs in the next train section, throwing him off his focused concentration.

Everyone was happy and smiling, like they didn't have a care in the world. The carol was in French, but he recognized it. *Silent Night.* Of course, it would have to be one of Dionora's all-time favorites.

And, of course, he knew that about her. She loved to sing, even though she couldn't carry a tune.

They reached her cabin, and Alexander took a deep breath as he reminded himself that tonight was probably more about torturing him than anything else. He raised his hand to knock on the door, but Stephan stopped him.

"You believe Dionora hates you."

They did have some rather nice talks over the last few days, but, using her words: *the kiss was a mistake.*

"Naturally, she hates me."

Stephan placed his hand on his best friend's shoulder.

"What's the opposite of love?"

He wasn't in the mood for a vocabulary quiz. He was nervous, but decided to answer because it allowed him to stall at the door for another minute. "I believe hate is the opposite of love. Why?"

Shaking his head, Stephan said, "Nope. Not even close."

Alexander thought of the emotional spectrum, and to him, hate and love were polar opposites. Always had been. "Of course, hate is the opposite of love."

"Hatred still means that you care about the person. Their opinion matters to you. Them being in the same room with you, matters to you. Whether they are alive or dead, matters to you. Otherwise, they wouldn't get under your skin."

Alexander supposed that on some level that was true. "It's still not love if they can't stand being near you."

"The opposite of love is indifference. That's when you know you've lost her. When she just doesn't care at all. When you truly mean nothing to her."

Alexander had never considered that before. But it may be easier for her to reject him if she *did* hate him. Maybe it was best for everyone involved. At this point, he really didn't know anymore.

"Love and hate have one thing in common." He didn't give his friend time to answer. Stephan tapped him on the chest in what Alexander assumed was his way of making a bolder point. "Passion. People will do the unthinkable for both emotions. They'll even kill or die for them."

Alexander had never thought of passion being associated with hate before, only love. It did make sense.

"People can flip from love to hate, and vice versa, in an

instant." Stephan pulled a small bag out of his pocket. "Just in case."

Alexander took the bag and looked inside. "Condoms?"

"In case this chaste night isn't quite so chaste. Remember, she's at her base age and could be fertile."

That was a good point. The last time they had been intimate, she was too young to conceive since vampire women were infertile until they transitioned during their Jahrling year. He placed the bag, which he knew would remain closed, in his robe pocket.

"If you don't use those, this is probably going to be the most frustrating night of your life."

Stephan's voice was filled with worry, which prompted Alexander to ask, "Why do you say that?"

"Oh, I'm not going to ruin her night." He knocked on the door and walked away with a concerned expression on his face. "Answer all of her questions. She's in a reasonably good mood. I'll see you in the morning."

Dionora opened the door leading into the tiny train compartment, and Alexander's breath left him in a rush.

She wore a white peignoir with lace trim. The two buttons on top fought to keep themselves fastened, stretching the silk fabric across her bosom and showing the matching white nightgown beneath. Her hair cascaded down, naturally framing her face. She looked like a bride in the outfit. White and pure. Ready to be unwrapped by her husband.

A husband he would never be to her.

He swallowed the lump in his throat and barely squeaked out, "You look beautiful."

Her radiant smile completed the ensemble. "Come in."

CHAPTER 17

*A*lexander studied the smile on Dionora's face. It didn't look mischievous, but then again, it didn't look innocent either. "Stephan said you were in a good mood."

And a good mood meant more trials.

Alexander glanced at the entrance, taking a good look at the door frame for any booby-traps. Once his hand did a cursory check and found no wires, he cautiously walked into the tiny room, his massive size nearly filling the space.

The train jostled him, and he fell into Dionora, who caught him between the lowered bed and the small dresser. Her hand held tightly to his chest as she steadied him, her body mere inches from his own. Her perfume—musky and seductive—tantalized him.

Glancing at her smile, he figured he was due for some torture. And he could pay the penance. His foot slid against a suitcase to give himself more room, but the weight of the luggage surprised him.

"This is insane," Alexander said, looking around and finding only about five feet of walkable area—and that space contained her—and more heavy suitcases than was necessary. The train had sleeper cars with berths, and this room was only one step above that. "Surely, there were suites available."

"This is cozier."

Cozier or crazier? He was going to bet on the latter.

"And you bought pajamas." Her hand slipped into his slightly opened robe to reveal the blue silk pajamas beneath. "You found my favorite color."

The smooth silk was already playing havoc with his senses, but to have her touching him? Each finger felt like a lightning rod to his manhood, causing the pajama bottoms to tent outward toward her. Looking into her eyes, which twinkled in concert with the huge smile on her face, he figured she knew exactly what she was doing.

"Three stores around town to find them and this smoking jacket." His hand traced down the robe. "All of it per your instructions."

"And you got to meet the tailor of the town."

"Mr. Eckman seemed nice." Alexander then thought back to all of the local merchants. "We didn't see the butcher or baker, for obvious reasons, but I swear the candlestick maker would have been next on your list."

She pointed to the top of the dresser where three candles stood. "I took care of that one."

He wasn't sure why they were talking about the towns-folk, for surely they were not on his bucket list of small talk for the evening. But at least it gave him something to prattle on about. At least, he wasn't mentioning how beautiful she looked anymore in her white silk peignoir. The fabric clung to her body, showing him her hourglass figure beneath. The scooped neckline was barely able to stretch across the perky nipples of her breasts.

The door remained closed to the tiny train compartment, allowing them all the privacy in the world. Alexander had not been alone with her—not like this— since the night before their wedding, and this small area that smelled of her perfume and her natural scent was starting to drive him crazy.

He became hard just looking at her. "What is the purpose of tonight?" His eyes burned, and he knew they were blackening with lust so he cast his gaze downward.

"Purpose?" Her eyes beamed with a certain coy twinkle to them. "To get to know one another. We're having a bundling night."

Somehow, that didn't sound as sexy as he hoped. "What is a bundling night?"

"It's traditional." She pointed to the tiny bed, and with her hand, she divided it in half. "You typically have a bundling board that divides the bed, but any barrier like pillows will work. The couple spends the night together, talking and getting to know each other, but there is to be no touching."

And now he knew what Stephan had been worried about. Alexander studied the bed. "I see no board, nor a row of pillows." He now thought of how narrow the bed was. "There's barely room for us on it."

She nodded like she had already thought of that and had a plan. "You'll sleep on top, fully clothed. I'll sleep under the covers fully clothed."

"Dionora," he said, closing his eyes for a brief moment. "This is not a good idea."

"Why not?" A devilish glint of defiance danced in her eyes.

Was she that naïve to think that he wouldn't want to make love to her? Or was she that determined to have him suffer? He assumed the latter, especially considering the outfit she currently wore.

He stared into her eyes, not caring if she knew he was lusting after her marvelous body. Perhaps that was all she needed to see in order to end the torment. "I am not lying on that tiny bed with you. Find another way to get back at me for what I've done to your family." He turned to leave, but her hands suddenly gripped his arm tightly.

"I'll admit, I enjoyed having you jump through hoops the last few days." A wicked smile crept up onto her face, letting him know how much she enjoyed the drama. "But, tonight is different."

"What makes tonight different?" He was afraid of what the answer might be.

She nodded to the bed. "Tonight, I want my old friend to talk to me. To answer some questions and,"—she eyed him with a hard stare—"be honest and accountable."

"Honest?" he asked, looking at her sheer nighty. "You keep throwing me mixed signals and torturing me for no good reason."

Her eyes blackened, and not in a sexy I–want–you way, which had him taking a step back. "I haven't even begun to torture you for what you did to me."

～

"I had no choice about the marriage," Alexander said.

"Of course, you did. I understand your need to honor your parents' wishes with their sire, but…"

Dionora bit her lip, and her face pinched. He could have ignored his parents' wishes. He could have stood up for himself and for their love. They could have eloped… So many possibilities.

"I attended your wedding. Did you know that?" She had never told anyone how she had snuck onto the private estate as a fake guest.

"You did?"

For a moment, his expression turned from anger to surprise.

"I needed to hear it with my own ears. You saying 'I do' to her…because you were saying 'I don't' to me with the very same sentence."

She thought back to that spring day. Between the two families, hundreds of guests—mostly vampires—had shown up. They filled the estate's northern lawn, which overlooked the family's vineyard. She had stood in the back and, even though she didn't have much of a view, could hear him loud and clear with her vampire hearing. Two little words that would separate them forever.

"How did you know what day the wedding was, and even where it was?"

Her fangs extended, and her hands balled into fists. "We still have mutual friends, Alexander. Some, unlike Stephan, remained true to me."

"I married Bianca. You know that. I fulfilled the marriage contract. You know that." He looked at her, and she could pick up anger in his expression, his eyes blackening as well as he stood taller and refused to back down. "What do you want from me?"

"I knew the day of your marriage, the day your son was born, and the day the relationship ended." She quickly did the math in her head. "You had fifty–one years, eight months, two weeks, and a day to come back to me. To beg me for my forgiveness for leaving me humiliated. But, no." She took a step closer to him. "Instead of finding me, you and Stephan were too busy whoring your way through the Balkan States, through eastern Europe, England, the rest of Europe, and finally making your way through Spain."

His eyes narrowed. "You knew where I was this entire time?"

"It was easy. You left a wake of heartbreaks in your path." She stood taller, matching his aggressive stance. "How many women did you sleep with? How many of them believed you loved them, only to be tossed aside as I was?"

"I never loved any of them."

Her eyes narrowed, and all she wanted to do was slap him. "You spent enough time in their arms and between their legs. It's no wonder you didn't have time to come back to me."

"Come back to you? You hated me." A low, guttural growl escaped his throat. "You *still* hate me."

"Hate you? I despise you." She shoved him away by hitting his shoulders hard, causing him to step back. "The only person I hate more than you is myself, for ever loving you."

She pushed him again, getting him closer to the door. "I loved you with my whole heart and being, and you tossed me aside. No one has ever made me feel the way you did. The way I still feel about you. The way I still love..." She bit her lip, her expression hardening as she looked at him. "You should go."

"Dionora..."

"Go, because I can't bear to look at you anymore!"

CHAPTER 18

*A*lexander stood by the door, his hand gripping the cold doorknob, but never taking his eyes off her. He had known how much he had hurt Dionora, but to see the hatred in her eyes, to hear her harsh words...it was too much.

"I have nowhere to go," he said, knowing how true the statement was. His family was merely his puppet masters. There was no one to love him, nobody who wanted to be with him.

"Find another cabin, stay the night with Stephan. I don't care," Dionora spat out the words through her fangs.

"I have nowhere to go. No one who cares for me," he repeated, the words sinking in. "My whole life has been wasted."

"That's not my fault. We could have had a life together, but you made it clear to me that you didn't want me, even after your marriage contract had ended."

He needed her to listen, so he stepped away from the

door. "I didn't seek you out because I didn't want to hurt you anymore. Hurting you was the greatest mistake of my life, and it has haunted me every day. The look in your eyes that day I told you I was marrying Bianca...I've never forgotten how hurt you were." He bit his lip, his extending fangs grazing his skin. "That look haunts me."

"Yeah. You were the victim." She moved in until she was inches from him. "Declaring me a whore because I wasn't a virgin for your marriage bed? Making sure I was unfit for any other man? That was..."

"That was my parents. I told them you had only ever been with me, but that didn't matter."

"It mattered to me!"

Tears welled up in his eyes. This was why he had never come after her. Why he never wanted to confront her again. There was too much pain.

He leaned in, her breath brushing against his face. "You're still the one I think of. Every day."

"I'm sure you think of me as you lay with your whores."

He took a deep breath, inhaling the scent of her, his body reacting and stiffening below in his pajama bottoms at just being near her once again. "You're still the one I dream of."

"I hope it's only nightmares."

He touched her hand and swallowed hard. Everything was on the line, everything that ever meant anything to him. "You're still the one I love."

She took a step back, closing her mouth, no longer baring her fangs at him.

"I don't know how you can stand being near me. How

you can even look at me for what I've done to you. But I have spent my entire life loving you and wanting to be with you, knowing that there is no way you'd ever take me back."

For a long, quiet moment, he stared into her blackened eyes, wanting so desperately to read her thoughts.

"You still love me?" she asked, her expression softening.

His eyes watered, and he didn't want to hear that she was still playing with his heart. "I do." When there was another moment of silence, he asked the one question he had wanted to know the answer to since seeing her in her office days ago. "Do you still love me?"

She stared intently into his eyes. It seemed like an eternity before she answered.

"I agreed to be your wife." Her voice broke and her tone softened. Her eyes filled with what he could only assume was love.

She had agreed to be his wife. But if she wanted to reject him, why didn't she get it over with? Unless... His heart beat faster, and he could hardly breathe. There was no way. "Do you truly want to be my wife?" he asked with a hint of hope in his voice.

She wiped away a tear and stared at the ground. "I've always loved you."

"Then marry me."

Gazing up at him, she said, "I don't want to be hurt again."

"I was a fool. I'll never hurt you again."

She tentatively touched his chest, and for a moment, he thought she'd knock him back into the door. Instead, her hand trailed down the silk pajamas, loosening the robe's belt, and moved down to his pajama bottoms, where she found his hardened length. Her fingers curled around the heavy rod, shooting jolts of pleasure throughout his body. "I've always wanted to be your wife."

CHAPTER 19

The scent of her arousal hit the air, and Alexander recognized her sweet aroma immediately. He looked deeply into her eyes and saw the blackened irises of a vampire who wanted to mate, not kill him.

"I want you to make love to me." She rubbed his hardened length one more time and then her lips found his.

The passionate kiss enveloped him, and his hands roamed her body with him first touching her back and then moving to her bottom where he pinched the two rounded cheeks before he pushed her against his erection.

The bed now didn't seem too small. He picked her up, tripped on one of the suitcases, but made his way to the bed, his back hitting the sheets, allowing her to straddle him.

He reached below the hemline of her nightgown and raised it up toward the round curves of her firm bottom. She wore no underwear, just her soft skin for him to touch. Rather than taking her garments off, he caressed and firmly held her backside until he could barely contain himself.

A gasp escaped her lips. "Rip it."

He tore at the peignoir and gown, knowing full well that her beautiful, bare ass lay exposed to the air, wanting to be touched. He continued ripping the outfit, exposing her back and shoulders.

His hands danced across her smooth skin, and the smell of her arousal was even stronger. He pulled her hair to one side so he could see her face. Her blackened eyes and extended fangs showed her desire. He asked the one thing of her that he had never asked of Bianca. "Bite me?"

She leaned in and plunged her fangs into his neck, claiming him and sending waves of delight through his body. His hands caressed her smooth skin, and he held the backs of her upper thighs just below her bottom, tightly pressing her against his erection as he began to rock under her.

He needed to be inside her. The sensation made his blood boil, but he held her more tightly until she was done marking him.

With all his might, he flipped them over on the bed, losing the torn fabric of her nighty in the spin. He laid his hands against her breasts and began to knead the globes in the palms of his hands. Her perky nipples greeted him eagerly as she arched her back on the tiny mattress.

"You're so beautiful." He pulled away, just enough to rip off his pajamas.

Now, with her legs astride his hips, he had full access to her. He had never pleasured her like this before, but with age came experience. He nibbled his way down her tight waist and across her thighs to her glistening core.

"I'm so wet for you." She spread her legs apart even further, giving him the view and access he wanted.

He placed his tongue around her nub, and her back arched. He licked along her slick folds and pleasured her by circling her most sensitive spot with his tongue and then gently sucking. His hands cupped her bare bottom as he lapped up her sensual essence.

She growled his name, not caring if everyone in the train heard them. Her legs spread out and lifted into the air as though she couldn't open wide enough to accept the pleasure he was giving her.

Her body rocked, and she placed her hands on the back of his head. "Oh… God. Yes! Right there." She rode his tongue until she gushed her juices and screamed his name once again.

All these years, and her body still melted when he touched her.

"That was…" she said between breaths. "That was new." She managed to give a thumbs up, and with a satisfied, heavy tone, said, "I approve."

A rough–and–tumble, tomboy of a girl, who was in every way a woman. She was the whole package. "I like the sexy talk. That's new."

"I'm a dirty girl." She gave him a sly grin and winked.

Damn, she was sexy. He needed to dive into her. He shifted his weight to halfway sit up, but her knee blocked his way.

"Uh–uh. You're not done down there." She placed her knee flush on the mattress and stared at her inner thigh.

It was an invitation, one that he had waited decades for. He licked up the inside of her leg, which caused her to shudder, and then he bit her high on the thigh.

The hitching of her breath filled his ears as he claimed her. Her blood filled his mouth and coated his tongue. It was only a taste, but a mark like this on the thigh was reserved for only husbands. It was a bite he'd never gotten to give her when they were first together all those years ago. Having lost her virginity to him before the marriage bed, she had wanted to wait for the love bite until their wedding night. The night that had never come.

It was the love bite he would give her every night for the rest of their lives if she let him.

He sealed the bite with his tongue and licked up her waist, kissing her belly button and nibbling up to her breasts. He then knelt on the bed and reached for his robe on the floor. He opened the bag and put on a condom. He had dreamed of this night for decades, and he didn't want the moment to end too quickly. He needed to slow down, to savor it.

She stared at the condom he wore. "You were sure of yourself," she said, the tone of her voice questioning.

"Stephan gave it to me. He's always so helpful."

She smiled back at him. "I'll have to thank him later."

He touched her graceful face, allowing his fingers to put aside her loose curls. He then kissed her on the cheek, then her neck, finally arriving at her full lips.

The soft kiss deepened into a demanding embrace. Her arms wrapped around his back as he lay atop her and gently entered her core.

He stretched her by pushing himself all the way in to the hilt of his manhood. Her tight body hugged his rod with every inch he gave her.

Given the way her body gripped him, he knew she hadn't been with a man for a long time. "I love you," he said, slightly pulling out and then plunging back into her. "I've always loved you."

A moan escaped, but she managed to say, "I love you, too. God help me I shouldn't, but I do."

Making love to her felt right. It felt like no time had passed and nothing stood between them. He quickened his pace and dove in again and again until his entire body tightened, and he felt his release.

He smiled and then kissed her nose, then her cheek... finally resting his lips against her neck. "It's always been just you in my heart, Dionora."

Her hand gently caressed his back, and she smiled at him. "Yeah, I've always been your girl." She gave him a wicked smile. "*Your* dirty girl."

He lay next to her, not wanting the moment to end. "I have a plan." He turned to face her, their bodies still entwined.

"A plan?" Her half-shut lids hid her eyes somewhat, but she still stared at him lovingly.

"Money, actually. And land." He kissed her cheek. "We can make it work."

She opened her eyes. "What are you talking about?"

He caressed her bottom and pulled her atop him, allowing her head to rest on his chest. "My parents will more than likely reject you. Your family's finances are worse now than they were when we were first engaged. But, I have some land that my parents don't know about. I can transfer it into your name. I can even open a bank account with enough money that, on paper, will make you more presentable."

He was worried that she would take offense, but, instead, she lifted her head and smiled at him. "We have lived in a world that has had two World Wars, a world that has barely known about electricity to rockets that go to space...." She smiled down at him. "We're not kids anymore. Does it matter whether we get your parents' approval?"

He had lived with money his entire life and was still unhappy. She had lived with no money and had always managed. He wanted to marry her regardless of the finances, no matter the prestige, and whether their parents approved or not.

He spun her back on the bed, ready for round two. "We don't even have to invite them to the wedding."

CHAPTER 20

"You told my parents we'd arrive tonight, right?" Alexander asked Stephan from the back seat of the rental car where he sat with Dionora.

"I told them exactly what they needed to know." Stephan turned down the wet road and drove through the rain. "They shouldn't be expecting us for at least another hour."

"I've never been so nervous." Dionora fussed with her ball gown, now regretting how frilly it was. The champagne gold Victorian ruffle gown looked stunning, and the color complemented her lighter-colored skin. But now her hair fell in her face, the ruffles needed steaming, and she had really only bought the dress because of a sale at a costume shop.

She looked like meringue atop an old lemon cake. The dress was so frilly Dionora had had trouble getting into the car.

Alexander fastened his cufflink and then held her hand within his. "You'll be fine."

Alexander would say that. He wore a classic black tuxedo with a satin lapel and trim. He looked stunningly handsome, whereas she looked like the next Disney princess. Even Stephan was dressed up and looking perfect for the occasion.

"Here are your masks," Stephan said, handing each of them a colorful face covering.

Alexander studied both masks before handing the smaller one to Dionora. "Is hers a peacock and mine a horse?" He gave Dionora a twisted smile, obviously unhappy with the selection.

"I haven't seen either of you in nearly two days, and now you want to complain about the masks?" Stephan grabbed the third disguise, which lay near him. "Mine is a giraffe. Do you want to trade?"

Dionora giggled and gave Alexander a sideways glance that told him that she had picked out the masks while still made at him. It wasn't a horse, but a donkey. But, if he thought it was a stead instead of an ass, she wasn't going to mention it. They couldn't get new masks at this time anyway.

Alexander glanced at the ridiculous giraffe mask. "All of a sudden, the selection back here looks good." Alexander set his mask down on the seat next to him. "At least the peacock matches your dress, dear."

Stephan inspected her dress from the rearview mirror, his eyebrow rising questioningly. "Isn't that the dress Belle wore from that Disney movie?"

God, it had looked familiar. It wasn't an exact copy, but now she knew where she had seen it before. "This one is totally different," she lied, accepting the brightly colored, feathery headdress. She put it on over the silk veil that covered her hair, but the feathers still tickled her neck.

Insisting that the reception party be a ball wasn't necessarily out of the question since Alexander's family had wealth and prestige. However, making it a costume ball was just another dig at their expense. Dionora had never expected to take the event seriously, and now, wearing a mask, she realized at least she could hide her anxiety.

"You're nervous." Alexander placed his arm around her shoulder and pulled her in tightly. "Just remember our plan."

She took a deep breath and looked at Stephan, who caught her gaze in the mirror once more. "Stephan will present us and tell them who I am."

"And once they reject you, I'll tell them I don't care about their money and that we intend to be married anyway." He picked up their entwined fingers and kissed the back of her hand.

"But first, we're going to get your land documents out of your personal safe, as well as your great–grandmother's diamond ring," Stephan said as he continued to drive down a road that felt familiar to Dionora—one that she hadn't traveled since leaving their old town in disgrace all those years ago.

"I don't need your family's heirloom."

"It's my ring, and I choose to give it to you. I certainly didn't want to give it to Bianca."

Now that Dionora knew what a terrible marriage Alexander had had, she felt more sorry for him than any anger for what he had done. She placed her hand atop his and caressed him.

Stephan turned down the private drive toward the iron gate.

"I can't believe your family still lives in the home you grew up in." She stared at the huge, iron gate as Stephan punched in the security code. "Looks like there has been some upgrades."

"This house is listed in the VTP."

"The what?" Dionora asked.

"The Vampire Timeshare Program. It's an elite program my parents take part in," Alexander explained. "The entry price is a two-million-dollar home or better to put in as a rotation for all participants. The idea is that a participating vampire can move into a timeshare home and look in their twenties, then, over time, adjust their eating and age appropriately over the next seventy years or so, then fake their deaths and move on to the next timeshare house."

"I had no idea something like that existed." And it was entirely like his family to be part of something as ritzy as that. Isabella would never live in a home that didn't cost at least that much money.

"They're nice homes with all the luxuries. Father put this one into the timeshare right after I married Bianca."

That was the second time in the car ride that he had mentioned his ex-wife. He had mentioned her three times on the train. She had been such a taboo subject before they had slept together. "Are you sorry that your marriage ended?"

"God, no." He stared at her. "Why?"

Why? "You've mentioned her several times in the last day."

"My life, to me at least, is divided into three sections:

before Bianca, when I was happy; during Bianca, when I was miserable; and then after Bianca, when I tried to recover from the terrible marriage and be a father to my son. It has nothing to do with wanting to revisit the hell I was in. And I certainly do not want anything to do with her or Enrico again." He looked lovingly at Dionora. "But I will refrain from mentioning her name."

She glanced up and caught Stephan's gaze in the rearview mirror. She shared in a lie, and it was killing her. Perhaps it showed in her eyes because Stephan pulled the car over and turned himself in his seat to face them.

"You do know that..." Stephan took in a deep breath, glanced at Dionora, and then continued. "You know you're not Enrico's father, right?"

Dionora felt Alexander's body tighten beside her.

"Alexander," Stephan said, "you're that spoiled brat's dad on paper, but not his biological father. I think the kid's blond hair is a dead giveaway."

Her gaze traveled from Alexander to Stephan and back, hoping that the truth would not tear their threesome apart, especially not now when they were finally together again.

A moment passed, and the rain pattered the top of the car. "Thank you for ending the contract and freeing me," Alexander said, his flat and distant tone hiding a secret, one she already knew. "For freeing *us* from that terrible hell."

Stephan averted his gaze by staring at Dionora, who merely shook her head to tell him that she hadn't shared his secret. He then looked at Alexander. "You knew?"

"I suspected." Alexander lowered his head in surrender. "I had no interest in her, and I knew you were..." He looked at Dionora. "I'd only been with her a few times during that last year, only to fulfill the contract. The timing was off, and I knew Stephan had started an affair with her."

"I understand." She didn't want to say that she already knew, but she had to start their relationship off with no lies, no hidden agendas, and no secrets. Of course, she didn't want to throw Stephan under the bus either, but she had to say, "Stephan already told me about how bad your marriage was and what he did to get you out of it."

He stared sharply at Stephan. "You told her?"

Stephan's eyes widened as though caught in a lie. He pointed an accusatory finger at her. "She was crying," he said as though that explained everything.

Alexander's head spun around so he faced her. "You were crying?"

"I've cried a river of tears over you," she admitted as she tapped lovingly on his arm. She never wanted to share with him how badly he had hurt her, but it seemed so unimportant now. "It doesn't matter. I'm fine now." She leaned into him more. "Let's just get to your parents' house and get this over with, because there might be more tears later."

Stephan turned back to face front in the driver's seat. "You know I can't handle a woman crying, Alexander. Especially not if it's Dionora."

"It's fine," Alexander said. "It's better that the truth is out, at least among us." He held Dionora tighter. "But that truth remains with us."

Stephan continued the journey down the private,

circular driveway and drove past parked cars that consisted of a Lamborghini and plenty of Porsches. Classical music played softly in the distance, and Dionora took a deep breath to steady her nerves.

The front entrance, with its courtyard leading to an expansive entryway with double doors lay ahead of them. "Drive to the back entrance. We'll enter through the kitchen and sneak upstairs to the library where my safe is."

Stephan drove around the house to where Dionora remembered the kitchen being. "Do you want me to leave the motor running?"

"Let's hope for the best, shall we?" Alexander got out first with an oversized umbrella and then held out his hand to assist Dionora. The three of them sloshed through the rain to the back entrance and walked in. Other than some of the catering staff preparing food for the human guests, the place appeared relatively empty.

Dionora held Alexander's hand as the three of them walked up the back staircase with its smooth, polished banisters and marble stairs. Once on the second floor, they walked past a series of bedrooms. Wallpaper now hung on the walls, a different color of paint had been used, and some different furniture lay about, but Dionora remembered the place well. The memories of playing hide–and–seek, tag, and running around this place as a child flooded her mind, and she felt as if she had come home.

They walked past the room that had been Alexander's bedroom, the place where she had lost her virginity. The home looked so different, and yet it felt exactly the same to her.

Stephan led them down a hallway where valuable paintings hung on the walls, and beautiful area rugs protected stone flooring. He was the first to stop at the double doors leading to the library. Carefully, he opened the squeaky door and led them inside.

"My safe is on the far wall," Alexander said as he walked into the room and Stephan closed the door behind them.

As a child, Dionora was never allowed in the library. Sturdy bookshelves lined the walls and curled around some lovely reading nooks. The nooks all held sitting areas, and she could smell the leather of the chairs and the crisp paper of the books along with the cool air coming from the air–conditioner.

The grandfather clock ticked as they made their way to a large painting of a man on a horse in what appeared to be a fox hunt. Since they were walking to the painting, she assumed the safe lay behind it.

"Surprise!"

Her heart jumped. All of a sudden, people were standing in the library with them. They must have surprised Alexander as well, since he dropped her hand.

Standing before her were Alexander's parents and a couple of partygoers in full masks and costumes. They had come from behind the sofa and some book–reading nooks.

"What is this?" Alexander asked, some nervousness evident in his voice.

Dionora wasn't ready. She'd known that she'd have to face his parents, but not like this. In a crowded ballroom wasn't better, but she'd thought she would have more time.

She needed more time.

"We wanted to meet your selected bride in private," Salvador said, his gaze now staring directly at Dionora.

Isabella walked over to Dionora, her hands out welcomingly. "Welcome to our home, dear."

"Thank you." Dionora's voice pitched high in nervousness. They were only nice to her because they still didn't know who she was.

She glanced at Alexander. Even though they didn't need his parents' blessing to get married, why was it that his family had always scared her? They were not very hands-on parents, but the mere sight of them always had her wanting to please them, and made her want to be the *good* kid.

Stephan walked up and stood between her and her future in-laws. "I'd like to present your future daughter-in-law."

"Dionora," Isabella said, not allowing Stephan to make the announcement. Her face held a charming smile that even made her eyes twinkle.

It was weird. Dionora had never seen her this ecstatic before.

Dionora removed her mask and the embroidered veil she wore, not sure why Isabella appeared so happy to see her. "How did you know it was me? Did the Council tell you?"

"Stephan told us," Salvador said. "He even told us to meet the three of you in the library before the party got underway."

Alexander and Dionora both shot Stephan a cold stare.

"Don't be upset with him," the costumed lady said,

walking towards them, her voice very familiar to Dionora.

"Mom?"

The couple removed their masks, revealing them to be Dionora's parents.

Dionora had left them in Paris. Plus, they hated the Marino family. She arched an eyebrow. "What are you doing here?"

"We invited them to your engagement party, and flew them out so they could be here when you arrived." Isabella looked over at Alexander and gave him an approving smile. "She is still as lovely as ever."

"Wait," Alexander said, his expression filled with confusion. "What is going on?"

"My dear," Isabella said, now reaching out and taking Alexander's hands in her own. "Ever since your father's accident, we've come to realize just how important it is to have someone to share your life with." She glanced lovingly at Salvador. "I almost lost him, and it occurred to me that you lost your true love because we were stubborn."

"You suffered for years in your first marriage," Salvador said. "We want you to be happy. And you were never happier than when you were with Dionora."

"So they found us," Gisele said. "Nearly a year ago now, and they asked if Dionora was happy and if we thought she'd be interested in marrying Alexander."

Dionora thought back. Her parents had asked her quite a bit about her job in Canada, her happiness, if she'd be willing to come to France. "So you convinced me to come to Paris and take a new job, and this was all apart of a bigger plan?"

"We had some hatred to work through, but we saw their point about getting you two back together," Ricold said. "You were never happier than when you were with Alexander."

"But we really couldn't have pulled it off without Stephan," Isabella said, now turning to face him. "He did most of the work."

"You manipulated me?" Alexander asked, his gaze studying his best friend. "I didn't know you had it in you."

"You were still in love with her, and when your parents asked for my help, I knew I had to pitch in and get Dionora's name on your bridal list."

Dionora stared at Stephan and shot him a disbelieving gaze. "But you didn't know I worked at the Verheirates Schlange. In fact, I only just started working there."

"I pulled some strings," Salvador said. "I got you that job."

He got me the job? A high turnover rate existed for her position, and she assumed that she'd gotten her job on her own merits. "But you wouldn't have known that I would put my name on the list."

"You put your name on my list?" Alexander gave Stephan an all–knowing glance. "*She* was the bonus name added to the list. I told you."

She gave Alexander a sheepish look. "The computer didn't match us up, and I wanted some revenge." The truth was out, but this certainly seemed like a day for letting secrets free.

"I was there to make sure you were either on the list, or that Alexander rejected the list and asked you to marry him directly." A wicked smile crossed Stephan's face, and his eyes lit up. "I must say, you adding your name to the selection made my task so much easier."

She studied Stephan's wide grin, and then it occurred to her. "There *are* direct routes from Paris to Venice by train. You booked us on a romantic sight–seeing tour."

"Initially, I was going to place you in the honeymoon suite on the train, but then I liked your idea so much better." He grinned at Alexander. "Close quarters. Nice and tight. I knew the two of you would either kill each other or admit that you were both in love." He then glanced at her parents. "Plus, I had to make sure your parents arrived before we did."

Alexander reached over and held Dionora's hand. "That was a tricky and risky game." He reached up his hand and kissed the back of hers, their fingers entwined. "But one that worked out."

"And we were to encourage you to marry him," Gisele said, directing her statement to her daughter. "Oh, it was hard because we couldn't just be happy that it was Alexander again."

"I think we pulled it off, especially with the pig." Ricold thumped his chest with his hand. "Who knew we were such good actors?"

Her parents had lied and manipulated her. Oh, their hearts were in the right place, and she couldn't complain about the outcome, but she never would have seen this coming—especially teaming up with Isabella and Salvador.

Giselle let out a slight chuckle. "Your poor brother. We didn't tell him about any of this until after you left by train."

That made sense. Dionora knew Edmund couldn't keep a secret. His wife Sarah was worse. One awkward glance in her direction and she would have spilled her guts.

"Edmund flew into a rage when he first discovered Alexander had proposed to you, but he settled down after the truth was out. He also agrees that you were your happiest when you were with Alexander."

"He couldn't be here?" Dionora asked.

Ricold answered, "He needed to be at the bar, but he does send his best."

"We want you and Alexander to be happy. That's why we're throwing you an engagement party downstairs." Isabella walked to a side table and picked up a tiny leather jewelry box. "Here is your great–grandmother's ring."

Alexander took the box and stared at it.

"Go ahead," Stephan said. "It's the moment we've all been waiting for." He glanced around at the people in the room. "What we all worked so hard to get to."

Alexander smiled, and his face softened. He got down on one knee. "Dionora, will you do me the honor of becoming my wife?"

With her hand shaking, she held out her hand, her ring finger poised for its new sparkle. "Yes."

THE END

I hope you enjoyed reading this novel. Please leave a review.

www.reginamorris.com/destined-desire-info

. . .

To purchase the next book in the series, please visit www.reginamorris.com/sins-of-the-father-info

To purchase the first book in the series, please visit:
www.reginamorris.com/winter-wishes-info

ABOUT THE AUTHOR

Dear Readers,

I hope you enjoyed reading my novel, Destined Desire. Please leave a review at the retail site where you bought the book. You can find a link to all retailers at http://www.reginamorris.com/destined-desire-info

Please visit my website (http://www.reginamorris.com) for more information about my other novels and short stories. Feel free to contact me through my website, through my social media sites (see my website for the list) or by email at mailto:regina@reginamorris.com?subject=Email from fan.

I like to play games and have fun with my newsletters. Please sign up. Newsletter.reginamorris.com

By day, I work in a small cubicle as a computer engineer, but at night I write about vampires. I captures my creativity on the pages of my passionate stories. I write about vampires who can alter their aged appearances by the amount of blood they consume. One of my vampire series, Vampire Secret Service "COLONY", is about a covert team of sexy vampires who protect the President of the United States. This series' success prompted me to launch another series ("Vampire Embrace") that involves the same world, but about civilian vampires who live among unsuspecting humans.

The heat level differs from mild to hot in my books. My stories involving the Historical Preservation Agency and time travel are mild. My Vampire series and some of my contempo-

rary romances are hot. These hot stories have an age warning of 18+ on them. My contemporary short stories are mild.

I live in Austin, Texas with my husband and two children. I graduated high school in Germany and I attended the University of Texas at Austin, where I received a degree in Computer Science with a minor in math. After enjoying a career in software engineering, I discovered that writing is in my blood, and had to put pen to paper!

The opinions I express in my novels are my own. My stories are my own intellectual property. Copyright (c) 2012-2020, Regina Morris

Sincerely,

Regina Morris

ACKNOWLEDGMENTS

Special thanks to my husband and our children for their love and support; to my sister for believing in me and encouraging me to follow my dreams; to my critique partners, Jean and Pennie, for being with me every step of the way; to my editor Chelle (Literally Addicted to Detail); and my proof reader team. I also want to thank my beta readers, and street team. This book would not be possible without the support I have had from all of you.

is getting more complicated by the minute. As if working with a covert team of sexy vampires to protect the President isn't enough, he has to deal with his rebellious half-breed son, save the President from a crazed vampire, and break in a new director for his team since the last one, his best friend and the only human he trusts, has decided to retire. Why does his friend's replacement have to be the most beautiful human woman Raymond has ever seen?

Career military woman, Alex Brennan, is being offered the promotion of a lifetime, and with it a romance that she has desperately been seeking. Does she dare accept the position as Director of the COLONY, an elite group of deadly creatures of the night and risk a dangerous romance with a man who isn't even human? Together, can they save the President?

United Service (Book #2)

Amazon Top 100 Bestseller

978–0–9888222–6–9 (ebook)

978–0–9888222–7–6 (paperback)

Available as an audio book

Sterling Metcalf is a modern–day vampire who clashes with his father's antiquated ideals. Being the half–breed of the vampire Secret Service team, Sterling hates being the team's weakest link. He jumps at an opportunity to do some fieldwork rescuing kidnapped vampire children and is accompanied by Kate Spencer, the nanny of one of the children.

Kate is a purebred vampire with a secret of her own. Can Sterling put aside his bad–boy ways and woo the lovely Kate? Will Kate accept the advances of a half–breed? Together, can they save the children from a religious cult who wants to kill them?

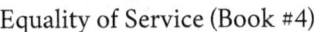

Enduring Service (Book #3)

Amazon Top 100 Bestseller

978–0–9914034–0–0 (ebook)

978–0–9914034–1–7 (paperback)

Available as an audio book

Vampire Secret Service agent Sulie Metcalf, the President's private physician, has been in love with the same human man for nearly thirty years. She refuses to allow herself the joy of true love because her feelings are unrequited by her human boss, Jonathan Dixon. As Dixon's retirement looms near, and his memories of Sulie and the last thirty years of his life are about to be erased, does she confront her fear of intimacy and take a leap of faith before it's too late?

Dixon has decided to retire and enjoy what time he has left. When his best friend Sulie, a vampire team member, is kidnapped during a medical emergency, Dixon realizes that retirement means giving up everything, and everyone, he's known for the last three decades. Will he risk his life, and his heart, to save her?

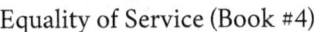

Equality of Service (Book #4)

978–1–948997–07–2 (MOBI)

978–1–948997–08–9 (ePub)

978–1–948997–09–6 (paperback)

Also Available on Audible

Fifteen years ago, Vampire Secret Service agent William Wardell met his future wife Jackie Pearlman. She's sexy, opinionated, and finds him to be a mockery of the American dream of equality for all.

Can a past Freedom Rider and racial activist from the 1960s, now turned vampire, prove to the love of his life that he's not a political puppet?

Reliant Service (Book #5)

978–0–9914034–2–4 (ebook)

978–0–9914034–3–1 (paperback)

Available as an audio book

After faking his death from an assassination attempt on the President, and retiring his first and only alias with the Vampire Secret Service team, Daniel Brighton discovers the mandatory sabbatical to be less than exciting. He chooses to do a favor and act as a security guard for a fading pop–singer, Lori Austin, whose career is winding down. He travels across Europe with her and discovers her past to be one of deception and intrigue with a history leading directly back to the team itself.

Lori Austin is struggling to keep her career alive, and is willing to do what is necessary to save it. From bad press and scandalous stories, she travels across Europe on a relief tour to revitalize her career, but doesn't realize she is traveling with a vampire. Discovering a hidden family secret, she realizes that the one man who can save her is the handsome security guard she fought so hard not to hire.

BOOKS IN THE "VAMPIRE EMBRACE" SERIES

These vampire romances feature vampires from the Vampire Secret Service world, but these vampires do not work for the government.

Winter Wishes (Book #1)

ISBN: 978–0–9981866–0–3 (ebook)

ISBN: 978–0–9981866–1–0 (paperback)

Available as an audio book

Sammy needs a holiday miracle. The Vampire Council is after him, he's falling in love with his best friend's mother–in–law, and there's artwork hanging on the wall that was stolen by the Nazis. Life is spiraling out of control for this Jewish vampire as he spends the Christmas holiday baking cookies and wrapping gifts for the needy.

Louise is busy with her charities and hosting her annual Christmas party. Putting a smile on her face proves difficult when her soon to be ex–husband arrives with a bimbo on his arm, her proposed divorce settlement is far from fair, and the sexy stranger she's starting to fall for believes she's a Nazi.

Destined Desire (Book #2)

ISBN: 978–1–948997–16–4 (EPub ebook)

ISBN: 978–1–948997–15–7 (MOBI ebook)

ISBN: 978–1–948997–17–1 (paperback)

Available as an audio book

After a car accident nearly kills his immortal father, Alexander rushes to his father's side only to discover that his parents want him to marry and stay closer to home. He's already been down this path once before with a less than desirable outcome, so he refuses. He's steadfast in his decision until his parents threaten to financially cut him off and he's forced to approach the Vampire Council for a new marriage contract.

Dionora is enjoying her new job at the Vampire Council Marriage Office. The holidays take an exciting turn for her when she discovers the next match she does is for her ex–fiancé.

Revenge is sweet with this sensual romantic comedy.

CONTEMPORARY SWEET ROMANCE SHORT STORIES

Taking Chances

978–0–9966192–9–5 (ebook)

Available as an audio book

Broken engagement, a disappointed father, an emotional mother, what else could a wounded soldier ask for? Tommy has no idea that his sweet nurse remembers him prior to his injuries. Always professional, Abby treats Tommy no differently because of their awkward past. Once the truth is out, what will become of their friendship and budding romance?

Christmas Joy

978–1–948997–18–8 (MOBI)

978–1–948997–19–5 (ePub)

978–1–948997–20–1 (Paperback)

Jake needs to clear out his father's old cabin and sell it. He's prepared to deal with the freezing cold weather and the remote location, but not with the sexy woman, who was once his late father's nurse, still living in the place.

More Than Puppy Love

978–1–948997–01–0 (MOBI)

978–1–948997–02–7 (ePub)

978–1–948997–03–4 (Paperback)

Ex-wallflower, now veterinarian, Kacie Preston is eager to go to her ten-year high school reunion where she can meet up with the boy she crushed on for years. But then his dog, her patient, shows up at the event mistreated. How well does Kacie really know her old heart throb?

www.ingramcontent.com/pod-product-compliance
Lightning Source LLC
Chambersburg PA
CBHW050940120626
46552CB00001B/302